Falling for a Pregnant Cowgirl

VARGAS RANCH BOOK 7

Karen Baney

desert life
media

Falling for a Pregnant Cowgirl: Vargas Ranch Book 7
By Karen Baney

Publisher:
Desert Life Media, LLC
Gilbert, AZ 85295

www.karenbaney.com

Printed in the United States of America

ISBN 978-1-960217-49-3

You rejoice in this, even though now for a short time, if necessary, you suffer grief in various trials so that the proven character of your faith — more valuable than gold which, though perishable, is refined by fire — may result in praise, glory, and honor at the revelation of Jesus Christ.

1 Peter 1:6-7 CSB

1

———

GABE BRAXTON TUCKED his ears under a beanie hat, the tips already cold to the touch. The scratchy texture chafed. He grumbled to himself, missing the familiar weight of his cowboy hat. But with temperatures hovering around minus four, warmth trumped comfort.

"Over here, boss!" his foreman, Ash Marshall, yelled as he flashed the spotlight over the bawling heifer.

Gabe parked his UTV near the first-time mother. He hopped out, leaving it running. The icy wind bit at his nose and cheeks, making them numb. Each crunch of his boots echoed sharply in the frigid air, the deep snow yielding slowly underfoot.

He watched as the heifer's abdomen rippled with a contraction. Part of the birthing sack poked out of her hindquarters.

"When'd she start?"

Ash coughed. "Not sure."

"Ash!" Gabe growled.

"Sorry, boss. The new guy missed her earlier. Could be as much as two hours."

Fool greenhorn. The words hung on the tip of Gabe's tongue, harsh and unforgiving, but he swallowed them down, the taste acrid in his mouth. The heifer and her newborn calf were his livelihood. Losing either would be devastating, a fact he couldn't ignore.

With their resources dwindling from the loss of cattle and other setbacks, neither Gabe nor the Broken Spur could afford more losses.

"Take her temperature."

Zeke Taylor, the guilty inexperienced cowboy, kneeled and performed the task. The almost-mama flicked her tail in his face. *Good. Kid deserved it.*

Not that the precarious financial footing of the ranch rested on Zeke's single failure. No, that situation was purely Gabe's fault. If he hadn't risked so much on his hairbrained idea to save the place...

Dad would have told him not to waste thought-energy on things he couldn't change.

"Her temperature dropped since we found her," Zeke announced.

Gabe exhaled, his breath turning into a fine mist in the freezing outdoors. Clearly, the heifer was in the throes of labor. He parted his lips to speak, but Ash's voice cut through the night air first.

Ash spat out several orders, knowing what to do. Gabe yanked his neck gaiter over his nose and cheeks, hoping to keep frostbite away. His stomach sank as he watched the mama strain.

If only they had coaxed her closer to the barn. He might have been able to get a vet out. As it was, the three of them were left to help her and the calf. He held out little hope of either surviving.

As the heifer's breathing slowed, and the calf was only half birthed, Gabe knew they were gonna lose the mama.

With a sharp tug, he ripped down his neck gaiter and yelled, "Get it out of her, now!"

Ash instructed Zeke on what to do. A harsh lesson to be sure, but one the young cowboy would never forget.

As soon as they freed the calf from its mother, Gabe stepped around them to clean it before wrapping it in blankets and setting her in the UTV's bed. He frowned as he passed Ash.

"You know what to do."

Ash's grim nod was answer enough.

"Zeke, you ride in the back with the calf. Keep her warm."

The cowboy climbed in the bed, shaking from either nerves or the cold. Once they were secure, Gabe drove them back to the barn, each minute ticking off in his mind like a bomb about to go off.

He'd give the calf a fifty-fifty shot at surviving if they could get it warm and nursing quickly.

When Gabe parked by the barn, he sent Zeke to warm up despite his anger over the mistake. Had to take care of the people and not just the livestock.

Then Gabe hefted the calf into his arms. Haydon swung the barn door open wide enough for him to enter. He hurried to the stall they reserved for newborns, the muscles in his back tensing. The calf's breaths grew shallow. She may have been out in the cold too long.

"How long was she out there?" Haydon asked as she followed him into the stall.

"Half hour on the back of the UTV. Heifer didn't make it."

His sister's mouth pressed into a thin line. As the oldest, she'd witnessed countless similar situations over the years, just like Gabe had. Each one seared itself into his memory, a dark reminder of the cycle of life.

"Go warm up in the office," Haydon barked. "I'll holler if I need anything."

Gabe grabbed a blanket for himself from the office before returning to the stall, tucking it around his shoulders. He saw his sister's disapproving frown.

It shouldn't surprise her. He wasn't leaving until he knew if the calf would make it.

"Mama."

Harlan's voice startled Gabe. He wondered how long his eleven-year-old nephew had been leaning against the gate.

"Is it gonna die?" Harlan rubbed his hand on his tented knee, foot propped on a bale of hay.

"Might." Haydon's calm response spoke of her hardiness as a seasoned rancher.

Gabe knew the truth. Despite her calm exterior, her concern matched his own. She just wore it better.

Better Harlan witness their challenges now, see the fight firsthand, understand the weight of survival — than step into a broken legacy years from now, blindsided by a failing ranch he never saw coming.

A fifth-generation cattle rancher. One day, the whole place would be his — if Gabe could save it.

And lately, that "if" had felt more like a desperate reach than a possibility.

After an hour, Haydon stood and play-punched his arm. "Why don't you go on up to the house? Nothing more you can do tonight. I've got this."

Tension coiled through his neck and shoulders. They could not lose the calf.

"This lone calf ain't gonna save the ranch, Gabe. You know it and I know it. You need some rest so you can start driving down to Arizona tomorrow. I'll be worried sick if you take off sleep-deprived."

Worried he'd die like their parents had. The words remained unspoken, but he knew she thought the same.

"Alright. You want Harlan to come up with me?"

"Naw. Be good for him to help me."

Gabe hesitated. His nephew stood in the glow of the barn lights, small hands gripping the gate, his young face too serious for his age. Good for him to see ranching wasn't just riding horses and throwing feed, but loss, sacrifice, fighting for something that might not make it.

Gabe's shoulders rounded under the weight of it as he trudged up the snow-covered walkway. The crunch of his boots echoed against the stillness, cutting through the chill. At least the snow had stopped, though the air still bit with sharp winter frost.

His phone buzzed. Ash confirmed the heifer was gone, said he'd made it back from the pasture.

Gone. Just like that.

Gabe acknowledged the text, then shoved the phone back into his coat pocket. He stepped into the ranch house through the mudroom, inhaling the familiar scents of wood smoke and old leather — the comfort of home, even as the weight on his chest refused to lift.

Toeing off his frozen boots, he hung his damp beanie, stiff coat, and gloves on the hook marked with his name. His gaze flicked to Vern's empty cubby beside Haydon's.

All the losses they'd endured.

He could not let the ranch become another one.

Scrubbing his hands down his face, he exhaled slowly. Haydon was right. He needed sleep before the drive to Arizona. His last shot at keeping Broken Spur alive.

Three years ago, their younger brother, Ross, had taken a job at Vargas Guest Ranch & Resort. He'd spent half that time hounding Gabe to come down and shadow the resort manager. Not the ranch manager, but the woman in charge of guest services, tourism, hospitality.

Not cattle. Not ranching. Not anything Gabe knew how to do.

He growled low as he poured a cup of coffee, the scent grounding him. Probably decaf, knowing Haydon — her subtle way of making sure he didn't stay up worrying all night.

He climbed the stairs to his room, the same one he'd lived in for all thirty-two years of his life. Only Haydon had switched rooms after marrying Vern, moving into the owner's suite, a space meant for their parents.

Sitting heavily in the chair beside his bed, he stared at the drained coffee cup, frustration circling the same thoughts.

Vern could have made this work. Could have charmed every guest, every skeptical ranch hand who thought turning Broken Spur into a guest operation was a terrible idea.

Because Vern had always been easygoing, charismatic, making everything feel like an adventure instead of a challenge. He had a way of drawing people in, setting them at ease, making them want to be part of something bigger.

Gabe wasn't Vern.

He was a rancher, not a businessman. A cowboy, not a tour guide.

Vern could have convinced people that Broken Spur wasn't just some fading ranch on the edge of Kalispell, Montana, but Gabe wasn't built for persuasion. He was built for endurance, hard work, getting things done. The thick callouses and tiny scars on his hands were proof of it.

Now, here he was, six weeks away from being forced into something unnatural, expected to learn how to be someone he wasn't.

Yurts. Guest lodge. Decor and smiling at strangers like ranching was just another attraction instead of a hard way of life.

The thought made his stomach tighten.

Life had taught him early that smiling was how people hid their brokenness.

You smiled, and no one poked and prodded at the scabs over your heart.

Didn't mean you had to be friendly. Didn't mean you had to mean it.

His faith had always been quiet, straightforward, practical, even.

You worked hard, made honest choices, and trusted that God would fill in the gaps you couldn't reach.

But lately, the gaps had started stretching wider, like the foundation under him was slipping.

Because the truth was—he wasn't sure hard work was enough anymore.

Tomorrow, he'd leave Montana behind for six weeks.

One more attempt to save the Broken Spur.

One more chance to figure out if he could change enough to keep it alive.

RENATA VARGAS EASED onto the seat of her golf cart just as Cliff wedged a foot against her rib cage, forcing a sharp inhale. The kid had no mercy.

She pressed a hand to her belly, smoothing over the taut skin where his movements made waves. Gymnast. Wrestler. Future black belt. Whatever he'd become one day, it wouldn't be from her influence.

Her latest attempt at keeping emotional distance was calling him by the name his mother had picked out—Radcliff. Raina, his biological mother and her cousin-in-law, had chosen the name to honor the man she'd adopted as her dad.

It should have helped.

It didn't.

Her head ached just thinking about the strange mish-mash of relationships involved.

A few years ago, Raina had married Renata's cousin Devon. Unable to conceive because of her endometriosis, Raina and Devon sought alternatives.

Following extensive prayer, heartfelt counseling, and discussions with her doctor, Renata had felt an undeniable calling—a purpose in stepping forward to be their surrogate.

She had been so sure. So certain it had been God's voice, His will, His plan.

But had she been wrong?

Had she mistaken her own generosity for His guidance?

The doubt had crept in slowly. First in quiet moments, then in restless nights, then in the depth of emotions she could no longer ignore. She had fallen in love with the baby inside her.

A decision that had haunted her for eight long months, filled with sleepless nights, gnawing uncertainty, and the crushing realization that letting go would not be as simple as she had believed.

Cliff shifted again, pounding on her kidneys. No mercy at all.

Pressing hard on the golf cart pedal, she barely noticed the crisp mid-March air or the soothing cool temperatures. Her urgent need to pee drowned out everything else.

She jerked it to a stop near the resort office, shuffled forward and promptly collided with a cowboy she didn't recognize.

Solid. Broad. A wall of warm muscle and firm steadiness against her fleeting balance.

"Whoa! Sorry," she tossed over her shoulder, hardly sparing him a glance as she rushed into the women's restroom, barely making it to the stall in time.

Renata exhaled shakily, pressing a hand to her belly as she whispered, "Take it easy on me, Cliff. We've still got a few weeks together before you meet your mom and dad."

The moment she said it, a wave of sorrow crashed over her, bringing tightness to her throat, burning behind her eyes, and an ache so deep it made her tremble.

She had prayed for peace, begged God to steady her heart, to reaffirm this was His will, but instead of comfort, all she felt was loss.

More than likely, Cliff would share those compassionate green eyes that both his parents had, that quiet steadiness Devon carried, that boundless curiosity Raina wore so openly. Would his hair be curly like hers, wild and untamed, or dark and sleek like Devon's?

One thing was certain; he wouldn't look like Renata.

Not her caramel skin. Not her deep black waves.

Not a reflection of her at all.

She wouldn't see traces of herself in the way he grinned, wouldn't hear echoes of her own laugh in his giggles. She wouldn't be the one he reached for in the middle of the night, the arms that rocked him to sleep when he was restless, the voice that soothed him through skinned knees and whispered lullabies.

She wouldn't even get to hold him after his birth.

Wouldn't feel the weight of his tiny body in her arms, memorize the curve of his nose, count the wisps of hair. Wouldn't be the one he clung to, nestled against her chest, needing her in a way that would never belong to her.

She had signed away those moments long before she even felt his first kick.

Renata barely made it to her office before the sobs hit, wrenching and raw, tearing through the fragile control she'd managed to hold on to all day.

She pressed a hand over her mouth, muffling the sound, then slowly reached toward her belly — only to hesitate just before her fingers touched it.

Instead, her palm hovered over the stretched fabric of her dress, trembling slightly.

Lord, watch over him. Let him grow strong. Let him feel loved every single day. Let him know You, seek You, carry You with him always.

She swallowed hard, forcing breath past the tightness in her throat.

And help me, Father, to let him go.

Her fingers curled inward, pulling away.

What kind of awful person was she?

She had fallen in love with her cousin's baby knowing full well he wasn't hers to keep.

Had she misread the signs? Had she confused loyalty with obedience?

Had she assumed that because she was capable, she was called?

Had she convinced herself that God had given her peace

when all He had given her was silence?

The tears flooded her eyes, spilling onto her cheeks like a monsoon flash flood, pooling into the hollow ache she wasn't sure would ever leave her.

Between sobs, she glanced at the clock.

Perfect. A big, ugly cry right before meeting Ross Braxton's brother.

Great timing. Just fantastic.

Someone's throat cleared.

The low, gravelly sound barely registered over the thickness in Renata's throat, but her body jerked in response, heat flooding through her veins as she twisted toward the doorway.

Gabe Braxton loomed there, not towering like her cousins but still tall enough to make her feel small, solid, looking every bit like he had stumbled into something he hadn't signed up for.

He wasn't wrong.

She felt like she had, too.

She hadn't meant to retreat, but the sudden awareness of him, the sheer presence he carried, had her scooting back before she could stop herself.

"Should I come back later?" His voice was cautious, edged with uncertainty, but his tone carried a firm weight beneath it.

Renata squeezed her eyes shut, willing the tears to stop, forcing them back like floodwaters against a dam.

"No." Even that came out as half a sob.

A beat of silence.

"Miss, should I get someone for you? Do you need medical attention?"

Her itchy, swollen eyes snapped up, sharp and unyielding, daggers nearly flying from her gaze.

Seriously. Won't miss pregnancy hormones.

She pushed herself to her feet too quickly, swaying slightly. His brooding gaze flicked to her unsteady stance, brows pulling together in concern.

"I don't need any help." Her voice was clipped, harsher than necessary, but she didn't take it back.

Gabe's grip tightened on his black cowboy hat. A subtle movement, but enough for her to catch it. A tell. A reaction to discomfort. His stance shifted just a fraction, but it was the kind of instinctive retreat men had when they weren't sure what they'd just walked into.

She had seen it a hundred times.

He was bracing.

Both his eyebrows inched up his forehead, dark eyes rounding slightly before settling into a look so steady it felt more like assessment than conversation.

"Gabe Braxton. You should be expecting me."

Braxton. Right. Ross's brother. Montana cowboy. Here to learn hospitality.

She was supposed to teach him hospitality? The thought nearly made her snort.

Gabe looked gruff. Rough around the edges. A cowboy through and through. There wasn't an ounce of guest services in his stance. Nothing about him suggested he'd ever greeted a stranger with a polished smile or a practiced ease.

Her gaze swept over him, taking stock as she had done with every employee that walked through her office door — even if he wasn't quite an employee.

Well-worn denim. Black cowboy boots, scuffed but sturdy, the kind that had seen years of hard use, not the polished kind men wore to rodeos to look the part.

That yellow plaid snap-front shirt stretched across broad shoulders, tugging just a bit too tight across his arms — arms that didn't quite belong in a hospitality role, arms that looked like they belonged hauling feed, breaking in broncs, wrangling cattle.

Everything about him clashed against the sleek, curated world of the Vargas Guest Ranch & Resort.

Renata's stomach fluttered — an annoying, completely

inconvenient reaction she blamed entirely on hormones and not at all on the fact that he filled out a shirt better than most men.

She bit down on the thought and shoved it aside. Good grief. Her thoughts were as scattered as her emotions.

She had no right to even notice his biceps, much less get distracted by them.

Clearing her throat, she extended a hand before realizing, too late, that the crumpled tissue was still in her grasp.

Gabe's gaze flicked toward it before he simply nodded instead, sliding his free hand into his pocket.

She narrowed her eyes.

"Renata Vargas. Pleased to meet you."

She forced a smile. It felt tight, unnatural.

He stared at her, his expression carefully neutral, but irritation lingered just beneath the surface, flickering in his eyes even if his tone remained deceptively calm.

"Likewise."

Translation? He wasn't pleased to be here.

Well. He wasn't the only one uncomfortable.

"Have a seat."

Gabe hesitated just long enough to be noticeable, just enough for her to see the wheels turning in his head.

"You sure you don't—"

"Sit."

He did.

Slowly. Like he wasn't convinced this was the best use of his time, but had decided to endure it, anyway.

Renata eased back into her chair, smoothing fingers over the gauzy fabric of her maternity dress, subtly wiping her damp palms.

She reached for her iced tea, taking a sip. Raina-approved decaf iced tea.

Whatever.

Her cousin wasn't here to nag her, but this cowboy was sitting across from her with furrowed brows and a presence far too commanding for her liking.

A presence she noticed more than she wanted to.

Exhaling slowly, she forced her face to relax and offered a smile that felt slightly more genuine but still required effort.

"Water?"

Gabe shook his head.

"Sorry, I'm a little scattered today." She set her drink down carefully, steeling herself. "Let's start from the beginning. What do you hope to get out of this engagement?"

The moment the words left her mouth, heat spiked in her cheeks.

Engagement?

She mentally kicked herself while Cliff actually kicked her from the inside.

"Oof."

Renata sucked in a sharp breath, stifling the reaction, controlling her face.

Feeling suddenly warm, she stood and crossed the room to turn on the fan, waiting for his response.

"You're pregnant."

The blunt words landed heavily, breaking the air between them with an almost audible crack.

Renata flinched, fingers tightening briefly around the chair's armrest, before she forced her posture into rigid control.

"I see your eyes work just fine," she shot back, retaking her seat.

She caught his gaze flick to her empty ring finger, his brow furrowing before his expression hardened.

Judgment. Assumption.

Her ire rose. Just who was he to cast looks like that? He didn't know a thing about her situation.

She jutted her chin in the air, narrowing her gaze. "Will that be a problem for you, Mr. Braxton?"

For a second, Gabe didn't move. Then he coughed, shifting stiffly, rubbing a hand on the back of his neck. "Not at all."

She held his gaze, testing. He didn't look away.

"Good. Then perhaps you can answer my question."

Renata straightened in her chair, forcing herself to settle. *Five o'clock could not come soon enough.*

2

—————

GABE HADN'T KNOWN what to expect, but the very pregnant, unmarried Mexican woman across from him wasn't it. Ross had left out a few key details, like the fact that his supposed business mentor was weeks away from having a kid.

Great. More complication. More distraction. More wasted time.

Still, he took her in, studying the contrast between sharp eyes and soft curves, her steady confidence despite the weight she carried, both physically and otherwise. She was small, built for control, carrying herself like someone used to calling the shots with confidence.

Intriguing, but not what he needed.

"When are you due?"

The words came out rougher than intended, but he needed to know if he had wasted his time coming here. She looked about ready to pop. Probably another thought he shouldn't say aloud.

Her chocolate-brown eyes flashed wide before narrowing sharply, irritation flaring in their depths.

"None of your business."

Gabe exhaled loudly, shifting back in his chair. *Touchy.*

"I ask because I want to know if I've wasted my time coming here. Ross assured me we'd have six weeks."

And as much as he hated to admit it, he'd need all six of those weeks, if not more, to learn how to run a guest ranch.

Her eyes darted toward the corner of the room. Gabe had spent enough years reading people to recognize hesitation when he saw it.

Yeah, she hadn't been entirely forthcoming with Ross. Not about to let that slide.

"The baby is due in four weeks," she admitted, voice cool but controlled. "My doctor says I need to take a few days off, maybe a week, before I can come back to work. During that week, you can shadow my sister, Solana. Or work with Dalton, the ranch manager."

A week?

Even Haydon, who was tough as nails, a ranch woman through and through, had taken three. And she hadn't needed stitches or bed rest or whatever else came with birth.

Renata looked nothing like Haydon, nothing like the ranch women who powered through everything without hesitation.

"This your first kid?"

Renata bristled instantly, and Gabe caught the fleeting strain in her expression, not the response of a woman excited about being a mother.

"Look, Mr. Braxton, I don't know —"

"My sister took three weeks off," he interrupted. "She had no complications, and she's a hardy ranch woman. Not like..."

Not like you. He stopped himself just short of saying it aloud.

Still, something about her situation didn't sit right.

"You're alone in this?" His voice dropped a notch, edged with curiosity. "Baby's dad just... disappeared?"

Renata's nostrils flared, but she didn't correct him.

Gabe felt something dark knot in his gut. *Of course.* Another irresponsible cowboy, taking what he wanted before skipping town.

He knew the type. Had seen it before.

Had watched it happen to Haydon, seen her struggle

alone, carrying everything on her shoulders while that worthless excuse for a man disappeared. Thank goodness Vern had rescued her. Had stepped up when someone else should have, had made sure she wasn't left picking up the pieces alone.

That same anger burned now. How many women went through this? How many men got away with it?

He let out a low scoff. "Figures."

Renata's entire body stiffened, like he'd crossed an invisible line.

Her voice was sharp, clipped. "Not everything is some cowboy running out on his responsibility, Gabe."

Her words had a bite to them, but what got him wasn't the tone. It was the way something surfaced in her eyes, raw, personal.

She wasn't just irritated. She was shielding something.

Gabe hesitated, just for a second, then tried to let it go. He still needed her help. Even if it was for less time than he'd expected.

Renata pushed her chair back and stood.

"Now, if you'll excuse me," she said, her tone turning painfully polite, "I'll have my sister show you to your bunk."

As she walked past him, her arm barely grazed his sleeve. Light, fleeting, nothing intentional. But for some reason, it hit harder than it should have, a quick rush of awareness.

Not gonna happen.

Gabe shook his head. He could not afford an entanglement with a pregnant resort manager, no matter how much she piqued his interest.

"What about my horse?"

Renata whirled around just before crossing the threshold of her office, eyebrows shooting up. "Why'd you bring your horse?"

Gabe shifted, suddenly feeling ridiculous. "For ranch

work. For riding?" He hated it came out more like a question than a statement.

She snorted. "You came here to learn the hospitality business, Mr. Braxton, not hire on as a ranch hand."

Heat crawled up his neck. She wasn't wrong, but it still stung. His reasoning had made perfect sense when he'd loaded his horse into the trailer back home—now it sounded absurd.

Renata didn't wait for his response. She pivoted sharply, leading him into the lobby.

A woman stood by the open front door, waiting. Tall. Confident. Familiar—but not in the way that put him at ease.

Renata barely slowed as she mumbled, "He brought his horse."

A slow smile spread across the woman's face.

"I'm Solana Franco," she said, her voice warm but laced with amusement. "Follow me in your truck, and I'll show you to the stables. Then the bunkhouse."

Gabe gritted his teeth as he climbed behind the wheel.

This place was already testing his patience. Too hot, too polished, too unfamiliar.

He jammed the start button, opening every window to let the heat drain from his truck, but the frustration stayed. March, and it felt like a summer furnace. A far cry from the frosty Montana winter he'd left behind.

He grunted, sliding his phone out of his pocket, thumbs flying over the screen as he shot off a terse text to Ross, venting his irritation.

Six weeks.

That's how long he had to endure this.

Guilt niggled, stubborn and sharp.

If Haydon were here, she wouldn't just give him grief. She'd call him out, straight-up, with no mercy, demanding he check his attitude.

She'd tell him to quit being a mule, remind him that not everyone owed him an explanation, especially someone going out of her way to help him despite having her own burdens to carry.

And worst of all?

She'd be right.

Gabe sucked in a deep breath, letting it loosen the tension between his shoulder blades as he released it slowly. His fingers flexed against the steering wheel, forcing himself to settle, to stop dwelling.

Then he spotted Solana in her SUV as she led the way. When they arrived at the stables, a tall cowboy jogged over to Solana's door and held it for her, a huge grin stretching across his face. The man leaned down and dropped a kiss on her lips.

Gabe's face scorched, and he glanced away as he shifted into Park. A poke of envy jabbed him in the chest. Would that he had someone that eager to see him.

He sighed, chastising himself for his foul mood. The sassy resort manager had one thing right, he had come seeking help.

What had Vern always said? Something about honey catching more flies. Whatever. He needed to get himself under control and into a better mood ASAP.

Swinging the door open, his short legs dangled over the edge of his seat for a few seconds before landing on the hard dirt. He stretched his neck from side to side before jamming his cowboy hat onto his head.

Then he heard his sister's voice in his mind, warning him to be friendly.

"Gabe Braxton," he said, holding out his hand with a smile. Probably looked strained. Oh, well.

The tall man took it in his calloused hand, pumping his arm up and down a few times. "Adan Franco. I see you've met my wife," the relationship further emphasized as he pulled her against his side, "Solana. She says you've got a horse to board?"

"Doubt Honeigh Bun wants to stay in her current accommodations much longer."

Solana giggled. "Honey Bun?"

"Honeigh Bun. You know. Like the sound a horse makes."

Adan grinned. "Sounds like there's a story there."

"Yeah, don't let your nephew name your horse." Gabe quirked one side of his mouth. He loved Harlan like a son and sometimes appreciated the name he chose. Helped Gabe remember not to take himself too seriously.

"Well, Honeigh Bun," Adan said, leading her from the trailer to the corral. "Let's see if we can't find you a cozy stall after a romp in the pen."

Gabe closed the gate on his trailer and hopped into his truck. He pulled it around to the side of the stables and dropped the trailer where Solana mentioned. Then he drove behind her toward the bunkhouse.

His nose twitched, and he drummed his fingers on his steering wheel. No matter what happened with the Broken Spur, he'd always had his own room. Never had to live in a bunkhouse. Wasn't looking forward to it then.

He cut the engine and joined Solana on the expansive, shaded front porch. The rockers lining it looked inviting.

"Ross traded bunks with one guy so you can have the open one next to him. Right now, we've got about twenty men staying here. The wing you'll be in is quieter. Ross thought you'd prefer it. Used to be my cousins' wing before they all married."

She held the door behind her, and he followed her inside. The entry opened into what he would have called a mudroom, a tiny space with several boot scrapers and a slew of hat pegs. To the right was a large entertainment room with couches, a poker table with folding chairs, and an enormous TV. Straight ahead, he spotted the opening to a kitchen, which he would explore later.

Solana veered left.

"This is your bunk. On the other side of the living room,

there's a similar wing, though more cramped."

"This'll do." Though smaller than his bed at home, he'd be fine.

Solana asked for his number and added it to her phone. "Dinner is served in the dining hall, right next to the office, from four-thirty until eight. It's included as part of your stay. Also, we'll need you to fill out the new hire paperwork tomorrow."

Gabe's head jerked back and his eyes rounded.

Solana laughed. "We plan to treat you like an employee, right down to the paycheck for your time."

He swallowed down an objection. Wouldn't hurt to have some extra money in his pocket. "Much appreciated."

"You think you can find your way around the property?"

"Yup."

"I'll leave you to unpack, then."

Gabe headed outside behind her, stopping to retrieve a duffle bag from his truck. Then he hung his shirts in the small closet allotted to him. He stuffed his jeans and other clothes in the tiny dresser.

Sitting on the edge of the bed, his mind wandered back to the spark between him and the spunky, very pregnant resort manager.

Something about her made him curious. Too curious.

She handled his barbs well, never flinching, never backing down. His mouth tugged upward on one side. The fire in those chocolate eyes. The vitality and life in her presence.

He dragged a hand over his face, exhaling sharply. No. He could not let her have space in his head.

She was pregnant. Due soon. Then she'd be a single mom, judging by the absence of a ring on her finger.

Even if he felt drawn to her, and he wasn't about to admit that he did, the last thing he needed was an instant family.

He had enough trouble keeping his own family afloat,

holding together the pieces of his sister's world, trying to be the steady one when everything else felt unstable.

Whatever pull he felt toward Renata? It wasn't real.

It couldn't be.

He blew out a breath, shifting his weight.

He just needed to get through the next few weeks, keep his head down, learn what he came here to learn.

Simple.

Right?

RENATA RUBBED HER arm where it had brushed against Gabe's, trying to douse the fire left behind from the contact. She liked the way his deep voice rumbled through her. And his intense, if troubled, blue, almost silver, eyes sent currents through her limbs.

It must be the pregnancy hormones.

Something niggled her conscience, much like the other Holy Spirit nudges she had experienced over the years. She ignored it. Then immediately felt guilty.

Lord, are you trying to tell me something? Something about Gabe?

Warm, fluttery feelings danced in her heart, leaving her even more confused than before.

When Solana came back, she found Renata wearing computer glasses, studying one of her many spreadsheets. Looking at the numbers without them penetrating her mind. She sighed and removed the glasses.

"Not feeling well?" her sister asked.

"No." A fresh thunderstorm of tears began. "Ugh. This is the hardest thing I've ever done."

Solana rounded the desk and pulled her into her comforting arms. The last of Renata's strength disappeared as she dissolved into another ugly, soul-wrenching cry fest. She missed the days of composure and joy — both feeling lost to her for months now.

Her sister rubbed circles on her back as her soft voice cut through Renata's inner turmoil. "I know this is hard. And I know Devon and Raina appreciate your sacrifice more than you'll ever know."

Renata's arms went limp.

"You'll get through this. Adan and I are praying for you. So are Mom and Dad. And the whole family."

"Thanks." Solana's shoulder muffled her word. She treasured her close relationship with her sister, even though it had shifted with Solana's marriage to a single dad. They were so happy together.

Renata stepped out of the embrace and reached for more tissues as jealousy crawled up her spine. The love Adan and Solana shared was special. Something she had longed for and never found. Almost thirty and walking through her first pregnancy alone.

A dark memory tried to poke through her conscience. It had been years ago in her early twenties when she thought she had found the one. Jace Tanner.

Of all the people to think of, why had he come to mind?

Probably because Gabe had commented as if some low-life cowboy knocked her up.

The irony was she had given that low-life rodeo cowboy her heart. Only her heart. She had hoped for something more. Something real with him.

Except she learned the truth. Jace Tanner was lying, cheating scum.

Renata expelled a loud breath. At least she'd found out sooner rather than later.

Oh, her life was so weird!

Raina and Devon had been highly involved through every step of the pregnancy, to where Renata wished they would leave her alone. But that wasn't the company she longed for. She wanted a husband, a home, and kids of her own. Like her sister. Like her five happy, thriving cousins.

Solana's phone pinged, and she glanced at it. "Looks like it's time for me to go pick up Jet. You need anything before I take off?"

She shook her head. Wouldn't hurt to leave a few things left undone in order to train Gabe the next day.

Heat flooded her face. The nerve of the man. Asking her about her pregnancy and the due date. He actually seemed mad when she told him the date.

Renata replayed the moment in her head. The way his jaw tightened. The flicker of something almost grim in his gaze. The way he had straightened, like the news had set something off in him.

Why had it mattered so much?

Well, good for Mr. Gabe Braxton. He could have driven down weeks ago. She thought Ross told him about the baby. Guess not.

She left her office, stopping to talk to Terri at the front desk. Terri was pleased to get a few days off for a trip to California. At least someone was happy with the arrangement.

Renata slung her purse over her shoulder. She stopped by the dining hall for a boxed dinner before heading over to her room in the small women's dorm, missing Solana even more.

For the longest time, it had been just the two of them in the three-bedroom place. Then Madison, her cousin Derin's wife, moved in for a few months before their wedding. Next, Raina stayed with them for a year, only moving out when she married Devon. Around the time Solana moved out, Terri moved in.

She sighed as she climbed behind the wheel of her white Jeep Wrangler. She'd angled the seat awkwardly so she could still reach the pedals but not have the steering wheel impeded by her baby bump.

The aroma of smoked chicken filled the space, making her queasy. She hoped it would pass. Lunch seemed like a year ago.

Cracking the window, she parked in her usual spot by the place she'd called home since graduating from high school over a decade ago. Then she grabbed the boxed meal and wandered through the living room to the back, to the sliding glass doors, onto the patio.

She popped the container open and sat down. After a quick prayer, she picked at the meal.

Loud laughter floated on the cool evening air from the direction of the bunkhouse, carrying easy camaraderie, casual teasing, the effortless way people could slip into joy.

She scraped a fork through the mashed potatoes, her shoulders sagging.

When was the last time she laughed? Or smiled in a way that came from her soul?

She shook her head. Months? Years?

Renata needed to stop thinking about the baby growing inside of her. Stop wishing for what would never be. Focus, like her sister said, on the blessing her sacrifice would bring to Devon and Raina. The child that would be their only biological one.

She closed her eyes, savoring the rich flavor of the smoked chicken. The fluffiness of the garlic mashed potatoes paired with the sweetness of roasted carrots.

Delicious food. Peaceful setting.

Then she opened her eyes.

As if she didn't have enough challenges for the last few weeks of her pregnancy, now she had to deal with a grumpy cowboy.

How would she transform him into a welcoming host?

She could see him now. Greeting guests with a snort, barely offering more than a grunt as he handed them their keys. Maybe he'd stare blankly when they asked about the restaurant, or Candi's Coffee Shop, or how long horse rides were. Or worse, he'd answer in short, clipped phrases, each word dragging from his mouth like it physically pained him.

Renata smirked. Guests would eat him alive.

She pictured it. A group of women, best friends on their last trip together before one of them moved away. The kind of group that came in all smiles, full of shared memories, ready to make the most of every moment. Gabe standing there, arms crossed, trying not to sigh as they asked about sunset rides, group photo spots, and whether the resort had spa services.

Then the inevitable. One of them would show up for a horse ride in shorts.

The sheer offense Gabe would take at the sight of bare legs on a saddle. If he let it go that far. Would probably send her to her room to change.

Renata giggled, just a tiny one, soft and fleeting, but more genuine than anything she'd felt all day. It lingered longer than she expected, a rare glimmer of light, foreign.

Then, as quickly as it had come, it slipped away.

She swallowed another bite of chicken, barely tasting it now, pushing the plate aside. Her shoulders rounded, the weight pressing back in.

Tomorrow, she would have to train him.

And tomorrow, she would find out if Gabe Braxton was just a grumpy cowboy with no patience for hospitality — or if there was something underneath all that gruffness, something that could actually be shaped into the sincere host his family ranch needed.

She wasn't hopeful. But maybe, just maybe, he would surprise her — in a good way.

Doubtful.

3

COWS WERE HIS thing.

Computers? Not so much.

Gabe expelled a loud breath, trying and failing to keep up with the rapid mouse clicks and keyboard strokes Renata blazed through. She probably thought she was going slow.

She wasn't. Not even close.

He'd only been at the front desk for two hours, and already, he felt inept. Bordering on a lost cause. All the peace of his morning ride with Honeigh Bun had vanished, replaced with blinking screens and an interface that seemed determined to make him look like an idiot.

Hours earlier, he had felt alive out there, free, watching the first hint of sunlight stretch over Dalton Peak. Out on the ranch, his movements made sense. Every step, every tug of the reins, every swing of a gate had purpose. Here? He was just a bulky, misplaced cowboy, standing awkwardly next to a tiny, clacking machine that was clearly out to ruin him.

He shifted his stance, resisting the urge to fold his arms across his chest.

Renata didn't seem to notice his frustration, or maybe she did, but wisely kept her comments to herself. Until she glanced up from the monitor, eyes flicking toward his face.

"You know, I think the scruffy cowboy thing is working against you here."

Gabe blinked. "What?"

She gestured toward his chin. "The almost-beard. The scruff. It's been, what... two days?"

He dragged a hand across his jaw, feeling the roughness. "Not intentionally."

Renata gave him a once-over, then shook her head. "You might want to shave before your next shift. We're running a resort, not a rodeo."

Gabe snorted, feigning offense. "Cows don't complain."

Renata huffed a quiet laugh, shaking her head. "Well, your guests aren't cows. And while I'm sure some of them love the rugged cowboy thing, most expect polished professionalism at the front desk."

Gabe muttered something under his breath about cows being less judgmental before Renata turned back to the screen, resuming her ridiculously fast tutorial on guest check-ins.

The computer's fan whirred too loudly, the keys clacked under Renata's fingers in a distinct rhythm, something effortless, smooth, controlled. He jabbed the keys with his index fingers, painfully aware of how stubby and uncoordinated his movements felt compared to hers.

"Gabe!"

His eyes latched onto her lovely chocolate ones, so dark they reminded him of fresh-brewed coffee. "What?"

She reached over, placing her thumbs at the corners of his mouth, her slender fingers resting lightly against his jaw, and pulled his lips into a begrudging, forced smile.

She smelled amazing. Like the first spring morning after a long Montana winter. Clean, new, something fresh woven into the edges of familiarity.

His chest tightened slightly, something shifting deep inside him. Heat sparked between them, sharp, fleeting, but real.

Maybe two seconds. Maybe less. But he felt it.

Then she dropped her hands to her side, too quickly, like she wasn't sure what just happened either.

"Looks like the muscles work."

Gabe swallowed, his throat suddenly too dry. What was that?

"Seriously, you will scare guests away with that scowl." Renata rotated her index fingers in a circular motion, mimicking a bright, overly cheerful smile.

Though it lit her face, the dimness in her eyes remained. Too bad. He bet she looked incredible when her smile actually reached her eyes.

A beat passed, and her smile faded. "Now you try."

Gabe forced a smile onto his lips. Just his lips. Not showing his teeth.

"This is gonna be a long four weeks."

"Six," he corrected her.

Her eyes narrowed.

He knew he was being a jerk, but he couldn't resist. He quirked up one side of his mouth.

"And now he chooses to smile."

Renata raised her hands in the air before letting them fall to her sides.

"Today," she said, straightening her shoulders, "I want you to memorize this." She handed him a brochure.

"Excuse me?"

"Memorize it. Guests want someone who knows about the property, amenities, activities, restaurants, and more. If you read words off the page to them, they're gonna feel uncomfortable. It will be a poor impression."

He sighed and stuffed the brochure into his back pocket. He'd read it. Later.

When Renata's lips pressed into a thin line, he shifted uncomfortably. Then the moment passed. A light smile graced her lips as if she decided whatever she'd been ready to say wasn't worth it.

Suddenly, her hand flew to her back, and she sucked in a sharp breath. Her features tightened into a pain-filled grimace.

"You okay?"

He reached out to steady her as unease coiled through his gut.

"Fine." She stretched the word for a few beats, her voice laced with discomfort.

"Here, sit in the chair." Gabe scooted it toward her.

"He's kicking. It'll pass."

A chime sounded as the door opened, and in walked a group of five women, wheeled luggage in tow.

The first had long blond hair that reached the middle of her back. She perched her sunglasses on the top of her head, her posture carrying the distinct air of someone used to being noticed.

Gabe swallowed down the rising bile.

"Smile," Renata whispered through clenched teeth.

He forced one onto his face. Then he scolded himself. He could do better. Had to, if he planned to run a guest ranch back home in Montana.

"Ooo. He's gorgeous," one woman behind the blond said.

Huh. Guess the smile worked. Maybe Renata knew what she was doing.

"Everly. Blair Everly."

Blair's voice oozed sophistication, cool and deliberate, as her eyes roamed over him, assessing, measuring.

Gabe blinked. What now?

Renata nudged his arm. He glanced at her, and she nodded toward the computer.

Right. Check-in.

He wiggled the mouse and clicked in the search box. His fingers found the E. Then the V. Then the E. R. L. Y.

A little spinny icon danced on the center of the screen.

Blair sighed softly. The kind of sigh that sent a clear message that this was already taking longer than it should.

He pressed his lips together, ignoring the way the back of his neck heated.

His eyes scanned the reservation. "Party of five?"

He sounded dumb. Of course, it was for five women. They stood there in front of him, their high-end designer purses dangling from the crook of their arms.

"Yes."

Blair's tone was brisk, her words precise, polite on the surface, but threaded with the slightest hint of impatience.

Gabe cleared his throat, grabbing the key cards. He fumbled with the stack, flipping one over the wrong way before swiping it through the machine.

Renata exhaled beside him, the kind that signaled restraint.

Heat crept up his collar. "Bear with me for a second. It's my first day."

Blair's perfectly sculpted brows lifted just slightly. "You don't say."

Renata groaned softly beside him.

He barely concealed his wince. Great. This was going fantastic.

At last, he jotted down their room numbers and handed them the key cards. He whipped out the map of the resort, scanning it frantically to point them toward their rooms.

His face flamed when Renata stepped in, smoothly circling the office, then the dining hall, and finally their rooms. No hesitation, no scrambling, just practiced ease.

She drew a neat line toward their accommodations, guiding them in a way that made Gabe's rushed attempt feel sloppy and amateur in comparison.

As the women headed out of the office, one turned back, eyes sparkling a little too much for his comfort. Blair's friend gave him a finger wave.

Renata hummed lightly under her breath, waiting until the door clicked shut before muttering, "Looks like your new girlfriend likes the half-beard."

Renata hummed lightly under her breath, waiting until the door clicked shut before muttering, "Looks like your new girlfriend likes the half-beard."

Gabe puffed his cheeks as he collapsed onto his elbows at the counter, his muscles aching like he'd spent the day hauling hay.

"You did good."

Renata's voice was softer this time. Not teasing. Just a statement.

Gabe hesitated, a flicker of warmth hitting somewhere deep in his chest. He shrugged, barely letting himself acknowledge it. Then he let out a breath he hadn't known he'd been holding.

"Ready for your next challenge?"

His stomach lurched like she'd kicked him clean off a horse.

Renata's lips twitched, not quite a smirk, but close. "Don't worry. It's nothing you can't handle."

Gabe exhaled sharply, bracing himself. He wasn't sure he wanted to know what she had planned for him next.

But he had a feeling it wouldn't be pretty.

RENATA HADN'T EXPECTED Gabe to handle Blair Everly's obvious annoyance half as well as he did.

Flustered, sure, but not overwhelmed. He had held it together better than she anticipated, even if he had fumbled more than once.

And he hadn't been flustered because of Blair's beauty. No, his frustration had been rooted in his own insecurities — his discomfort with learning something foreign, something outside his world.

Renata tapped a finger against her arm. A hint of approval mixed with the pity. He wasn't hopeless. Just out of his element.

It may have been a little indulgent to tease him about

another big challenge. But he had a lot to learn, and she had a lot to cover with him in the next few weeks. No sense going easy on him.

Allowing that thought to settle, Renata motioned to the door.

"We don't have anyone scheduled to arrive for the next few hours." She flipped the sign hanging on the glass door and locked it. "So what do you say we get some lunch first?"

Gabe exhaled loudly, his shoulders dropping, the tension in his frame easing just enough for Renata to see how much he needed the break.

"Since you're looking to replicate this on your own at home, here's something to consider." She tapped the sign, bringing his attention back to it. "We use this with my number and Solana's so we can take breaks. When we're fully staffed, we stagger our breaks. But if we have to leave the front office unattended, we make it clear how guests can reach us."

"Gotcha."

He pulled out his phone, thumbs flying over the keyboard with practiced ease, before stowing it again.

Too bad the reservation management system wasn't on his phone. She had a feeling he'd pick it up quicker.

Renata led the way to the dining hall, but Gabe's steps dragged—just slightly, just enough for her to notice.

His gaze caught on the inscription above the entryway, the cream-colored lettering catching the late-morning light, soft yet unwavering. She followed his stare.

The words stood bold against the muted backdrop—deliberate, permanent, meant to steady anyone who read them.

"We do not deviate from the Lord's plan."

Gabe muttered it under his breath, just audible enough for her to hear.

His lips pressed together briefly before he exhaled through his nose, controlled.

Renata angled herself toward him, studying his reaction.

A quiet huff escaped him, sharp and sardonic, his head tilting slightly as his eyes narrowed at the lettering — like he was measuring it against something unseen.

"Right." His voice was dry, edged with something unresolved. "And does He send that plan by express mail, or should I expect it to arrive in a burning bush?"

She heard it clearly now — the strain beneath his sarcasm.

His gaze dropped lower, skimming the verses beneath the motto.

Psalm 17:4-5.

With regard to the works of man, by the word of your lips I have avoided the ways of the violent. My steps have held fast to your paths; my feet have not slipped.

His fingers curled briefly, then flexed open again. A small, almost imperceptible recoil.

Renata caught it.

She said nothing. Just waited.

A beat of silence stretched between them, taut with something unsaid.

Then, without comment, she motioned toward the buffet line, giving him space to speak if he wanted to.

He didn't.

That, more than the sarcasm, told her everything.

Gabe Braxton was searching. Maybe for solid ground with his family's ranch. Maybe for something deeper.

Renata wouldn't pry. But his reaction stirred something familiar in her, something deeply human.

Because wasn't she trying to find her own footing too? Not just for the resort. For life after Cliff's birth.

She drew in a slow breath, shifting toward the mundane as she reached for a plate.

"Smells good."

Gabe's voice was quieter now, his focus shifting like he needed the distraction just as much as she did.

"Yeah," she replied easily. "Chef is amazing. He's been with our family for at least a decade. Maybe closer to fifteen years now."

"That smoked chicken last night—" His voice lightened slightly, like he was actively pulling himself from the heaviness of his thoughts.

His resilience surprised her, not because she doubted him, but because even in the middle of uncertainty, he didn't let himself sit in defeat.

That quiet determination, grit layered beneath frustration, stirred something in her she didn't expect.

She focused on the plate in her hand, brushing off the quiet admiration she felt before it had the chance to settle.

"Was amazing. Wish I had time to cook food like that."

Renata spread mixed greens over the ceramic plate, the crisp scent of fresh vegetables mixing with the hint of smoked chicken from Chef's efforts yesterday. She drizzled a chipotle ranch over the top, the creamy spice hitting her senses as she reached for a second plate for Gabe.

Renata spotted an opportunity. If he was serious about this guest ranch, food would be a crucial piece of the experience.

"Have you thought about food services yet? A dining hall? Cooks? A chef?"

Gabe's shoulders stiffened slightly, his frame losing its easy looseness. His gaze dropped toward his plate, a hesitation, a distraction, before settling again.

"I'm not sure where to start with some of this."

The quiet admission carried more weight than she expected.

Renata's fingers tightened around her plate. She recognized that look, the one people wore when standing at the edge of something too big to tackle all at once.

He didn't meet her eyes immediately, but when he did, hesitation flickered, like saying more might make it too real.

She could see it now. He was out of his depth.

Starting a guest ranch from scratch. Vendors, staff, rooms, renovations. It was overwhelming. No wonder he felt unsteady.

Maybe she needed to shift focus this afternoon. Not just teach him processes, but understand his vision.

Hospitality was only one piece. And whether he realized it or not, he'd shown her enough glimmers of hope that he could learn the rest.

Gabe cleared his throat and nodded toward the tables.

"You pick out a seat, and I'll join you. What do you want to drink?"

Renata hesitated, appreciating the offer.

"Water," she finally said, even though she'd rather have iced tea, the non-Raina-approved kind.

She took her plate, glancing briefly at Gabe before moving toward the doors, letting the weight of the conversation settle as she stepped into the fresh air. She found a shaded corner where the breeze carried the scent of sun-warmed dust and desert air, a soothing contrast to the energy lingering between them.

This was why she loved Arizona in March. Warm, but not suffocating, the kind of weather that invited quiet reflection while enjoying nature.

Last year, when her cousin Drake remodeled the kitchen and added a coffee shop bakery for his wife, she'd asked him to include a small employee-only seating area outside. He'd happily agreed.

Renata settled onto the metal picnic bench, exhaling as she bowed her head briefly.

Lord, give me wisdom to help Gabe in the way he needs the most help.

Because maybe her assumptions about these weeks had been off. She'd approached this like she was training him for her role at Vargas Guest Ranch & Resort. But she wasn't. She was preparing the cowboy to build something entirely new.

In Montana.

A hummingbird's buzz undulated as it hovered from one honeysuckle bloom to the next, its tiny wings beating faster than the eye could track. Renata traced her fingers absently over the edge of her plate, rolling through her next steps in her mind, wondering if clarity ever came as effortlessly as flight.

Then footsteps approached, quiet but firm, drawing her attention back to the moment.

When Gabe joined her, she flashed him a deeply genuine smile.

"Well, Gabe, I may not be your burning bush, but I promise you this. I'll make sure you don't feel quite so lost while you're here."

She met his gaze, considering him for half a second longer than she meant to.

Something flickered, an awareness, quiet but undeniable, settling into the space between them.

Gabe shifted slightly, his fingers grazing the edge of his glass, like movement might keep the moment from pressing too deep.

Then she began asking him questions, feeling certain this was why God dropped this handsome, overwhelmed cowboy into the middle of her resort.

4

I MAY NOT be your burning bush.

Renata's words hung in the air long after she'd spoken them, weaving themselves into Gabe's thoughts like burrs caught in the fabric of his mind—clinging, persistent, impossible to ignore.

They should have been easy to brush off. Dismissed as just another throwaway comment, something spoken with conviction but lacking real weight.

But they weren't.

Because she had said it too confidently, as if she knew something he didn't.

And the worst part? He trusted her words.

Maybe she was his burning bush. Maybe she didn't know it. Maybe he didn't want her to be.

Because if she was, it meant he had to pay attention. And that? That was dangerous.

He wasn't looking for signs.

Had spent months actively avoiding them, ignoring nudges toward the idea of picking up where Vern left off—stepping into something that had never really been his.

The guest ranch idea? That had been Gabe's. Just a thought, a vague suggestion tossed out in passing, a way to salvage the cattle ranch, to preserve the Broken Spur, the Braxton family legacy.

A problem with no solution, just an idea sitting on the

table, waiting for someone else to figure it out.

Vern had been the one to grab it and make it something real. He had built plans, gathered vendors, turned spreadsheets into blueprints. Poured himself into it like it was a calling, a vision meant to be fulfilled.

Gabe had watched, half-amused, half-relieved, glad someone else had picked up the idea he hadn't fully believed in himself.

And then Vern had died.

And the weight crashed onto Gabe.

Not as a dream he had been fighting for, but as a half-built solution sitting on his shoulders, unfinished, waiting. Waiting for him. Waiting to be claimed.

He wasn't Moses, staring down a flaming declaration from heaven. Wasn't some divinely appointed leader, meant to forge ahead with certainty.

He was just Gabe Braxton, a perplexed cowboy standing at the edge of an idea that had never really belonged to him, in a desperate attempt to save the place four generations had called home.

With expectations pressing in from all sides.

And yet Renata was here. And something about that mattered.

He wanted to disregard the thought, bury it under the practical, the logical, the safer conclusions that let him believe he was just here for six weeks. To learn from her. That was it. That was all it was supposed to be.

But now that his mind had made the connection that his time here could have something to do with her, it wouldn't settle. Wouldn't fade. Wouldn't let him go.

He dropped his plate onto the metal picnic table, the cool shade offering relief from Arizona's March sun. It wasn't suffocating, but it pressed against his skin, clinging with a dry persistence Montana never had.

A reminder. This wasn't home.

Renata settled across from him, reaching for her water

bottle. Before she could twist the cap, he beat her to it, unscrewing the lid and setting it in front of her.

Her soft smile flickered, brief, almost like she hadn't meant to let it slip.

And something shifted in his chest. Like pouring hot fudge over an ice cream sundae. Warm. Comforting. Inviting.

She tucked a strand of hair behind her ear, her fingers slow in the movement, as if she had caught the brief note of tension between them too.

He exhaled before he could think too much about it, burying the feeling as quickly as it settled.

"Why don't you start by telling me more about your plans?" she asked.

Gabe picked at the edge of his smoked chicken sandwich, tearing off a bite, chewing slower than necessary. As if stalling would make the answer easier to find.

The truth? He had very little figured out.

His grand contribution to the guest ranch idea had been just that—an idea. Not a plan. Not something he had worked for, fought for, put his heart into.

A suggestion. Something that had felt less like a dream and more like a desperate solution, one thrown out in an attempt to save the cattle ranch, to preserve the Broken Spur before it slipped away.

"Yurts."

The word burst from his mouth unexpectedly.

Renata's brows lifted and her head tilted to the side. "Yurts?"

He sighed, shaking his head. "Vern wanted us to use yurts. I didn't even know what the blasted thing was before he ordered them. Now I've got four of them I don't quite know what to do with."

Her lips twitched. "It's okay. You can laugh."

A small giggle escaped those pretty lips, soft and fleeting, slipping between them before she could stop it.

Gabe hadn't expected it. Hadn't expected to like it, either.

Focus, Gabriel.

Renata speared another bite of her salad, pausing just before lifting it to her mouth. Her brow knitted, subtle, thoughtful, before her gaze flicked to him, lingering a beat longer than before.

"Who's Vern?"

Right. She didn't know.

"Guess I should have started from the beginning."

She nodded. "Might help."

"Vern is my sister's late husband."

Renata's chewing slowed, her attention sharpening.

"We'd been trying to figure out a way to save the ranch. I suggested we tap into the tourist market in Kalispell. With Glacier National Park just miles away, we get a massive influx of international visitors in the summer months. And some tourists come just for our mountains and lakes never even visiting the park."

Gabe shoved a fry into his mouth and swallowed before continuing.

"Vern took my half-baked idea and ran with it. He started researching. Building spreadsheets. Ordering supplies. Making connections with vendors."

His stomach twisted. He pushed his plate away.

"Then he had a heart attack and died."

Renata's hand stilled on her fork.

"Oh, I'm so sorry for your loss. How's your sister doing?"

"Haydon's a hardy woman."

He wouldn't share the true nature of her marriage to Vern. One rooted in mutual friendship, one meant to provide his nephew with reliability, one that grew into love, her words, despite their twenty-two-year age gap.

"So is her son, Harlan. He's eleven."

"Oh, so young to lose his dad."

His shoulder hitched in a half-shrug. "Seems to be the hallmark of our lives."

She didn't rush past the moment. Didn't offer clichés or empty reassurances. She simply waited, giving him space to sit with the weight of the words.

After a beat, he exhaled.

"Anyway, now I'm trying to make sense of it all and get the thing up and running. We took out a loan, counting on opening this year."

"When does the season start?"

"June."

Her eyes rounded instantly. The reaction was immediate, a mirror of the anxiety winding tight in his gut.

"That's not much time."

"Tell me about it."

Unease crept up his spine, tensing his neck muscles. He exhaled slowly, but it did nothing to ease the pressure. His fingers twitched, restless, ready for motion. He needed to move, to break the silence, to escape the weight pressing in on his chest. Forward momentum felt easier than standing still, easier than sitting with thoughts that refused to settle.

"Should we head back to the office?" he asked.

"Sure."

Renata nudged her tray forward and eased to her feet, but the slow, measured movement told him more than words ever could. Pain, tension. It was there, wound tightly beneath her practiced posture. He watched as she took a steadying breath, controlled, deliberate, as if she refused to acknowledge the strain.

For half a second, he hesitated, expecting her to push through it on her own. To straighten her spine, adjust her stance, swallow whatever discomfort she wasn't willing to voice. But she didn't.

Before he even registered the impulse, his arm was out. Not tentative, not questioning, just there, offering balance without thinking about why the urge had hit so fast.

She let out a slow breath, accepting the steadiness without moving away, without pulling back, without pretending she didn't need it. Her fingers brushed against his arm, just light, fleeting, but somehow, that was worse than if she'd gripped him outright.

Because now he was aware. Of her. Of the warmth of her touch. Of the way the brief contact settled deep in his chest, uninvited and impossible to ignore.

Renata lifted her chin, meeting his gaze for a beat too long before looking toward the path leading to the office. "Let's go."

Gabe dropped his hand, took a step back, and followed her.

As they walked, her hand flitted to the side of her baby bump. Gentle, instinctive, protective. Gabe noticed immediately. He remembered Haydon doing the same, the absent-minded palm resting under her belly like it was second nature, like it was enough to shield something fragile beneath the surface.

A normal instinct. Maternal. But with Renata, it felt different.

She hadn't talked about the baby. Hadn't fussed over cravings. Hadn't done any of the things Haydon had when she was pregnant with Harlan. Hadn't even called the baby hers.

Maybe she was just one of those quiet types. Reserved, more internal. Still...

His voice came without planning. "Do all expectant mothers do that?"

Renata hesitated. Just for a breath. A flicker of something passed through her eyes, too fast for him to catch, before a flush crept onto her cheeks. "Instinct, I suppose."

The response was controlled. Too controlled. Like she'd thought about it before. Like she'd rehearsed it. Like she wanted him to drop it.

But now, he couldn't.

She straightened, just barely, her shoulders pulling back, chin lifting in a quiet defense. Her movements were measured, deliberate, like every step was placed with practiced ease. A subtle distance settled between them, the kind that wasn't physical but felt just as real. She was used to standing alone.

He frowned, watching the way she moved, the way she held herself, the way she didn't act like a woman preparing for life as a mother.

Something wasn't adding up. He wasn't sure what yet.

But he'd find out.

A THOUSAND PINPRICKS pierced Renata's spine, the back of her eyes burning as emotions surged. Her fingers curled instinctively over her belly, the touch automatic, unthinking.

Not love. Not anticipation of the baby's arrival.

Lies.

She loved Cliff. But he wasn't hers to love. Not hers to nurture.

She swallowed hard, blinking against the heat gathering behind her eyes. But the faint trace of Gabe's scent lingered as he held the door open for her. She ducked her head, hoping he hadn't seen it. The office door clicked shut behind them.

Renata straightened, exhaling slowly, forcing control back into her limbs. But when she moved, his presence followed—quiet, unwavering, never overwhelming, yet impossible to ignore. She blinked, clearing the emotion from her eyes before lifting her chin.

Then she reached for the stack of notes on her desk, needing a tangible anchor—a task, a purpose, a reminder of what she could control. Because she knew this role. She knew how to guide people, organize chaos, breathe life into plans that weren't her own. She focused on that.

Not on Cliff. Not on Gabe standing too close, his presence lingering at the edges of her awareness, pressing subtly against her senses.

She turned, keeping her expression neutral, professional. "Well," she said, clearing her throat. "Let's start making sense of this guest ranch of yours."

Gabe hesitated, just for a beat, just long enough for her to catch something unreadable in his expression before nodding. And then he didn't let it go.

"What's wrong?"

Renata's chest squeezed tight. She pressed her lips into a firm line, shaking her head. She needed him to let it go. Needed him to focus on his ranch, his plans. Anything but her. Anything but the little one growing inside her.

"Do you miss the guy that did this?"

Her gaze snapped to his, sharp and immediate.

It felt easier to let him believe the assumptions he clung to than to explain the bizarre, nearly unbelievable truth. Her hand brushed lightly over her belly with a fleeting touch, instinctive, as if answering some silent pull she never fully questioned.

She never spoke about the baby. Never called him hers. Because he wasn't. And maybe that made her reactions seem more strange to Gabe.

A quiet shift in the air pulled her awareness outward. Gabe was close, undeniably present, his nearness settling into the space between them with solid certainty.

"He still around?"

The question was quiet, but there was no mistaking the edge beneath it. She froze. The air charged.

Not from nerves. Not from fear. From the quiet weight of something she didn't dare name.

"Is he bugging you?"

The heat behind her ribs spread higher like something dangerous creeping too close.

"He hurting you?"

Her stomach tightened.

Then the stark truth stabbed her in ways she hadn't braced for.

She was falling for someone she couldn't have. Him. Gabe. His protective concern.

Her pulse pressed thick against her throat. She couldn't. She wouldn't.

Renata forced a slow breath, palms pressing against the desk, grasping for steadiness, for anything untouched by the dust devil twisting inside her. Before she let anything slip, she cleared her throat.

"No. None of those things."

She expected him to drop it. To take her answer at face value and move on. But Gabe didn't. He watched her, weighing whether her words held the truth.

Her fingers twitched over the mouse, searching for an escape. She cleared her throat.

"Yurts."

She typed into the search bar, avoiding Gabe's gaze. "I think I have to look these up, unless you've got a picture."

Gabe exhaled slowly. Finally, he spoke, his voice lower, the edges rougher. "Yeah. Yurts."

It wasn't a concession. Just an acknowledgment that she had shifted the conversation, but the tension hadn't moved.

Renata forced herself to breathe, fingers stiff as she scrolled through the search results on her screen. She could feel him watching her. And that was worse.

Laughing nervously, Renata asked, "You already have them? Yurts?"

"Yeah."

"Do you know the brand or anything? I'd love to see a picture."

Gabe whipped out his phone, his fingers quick, efficient in the same way he carried himself.

Renata giggled. "You're almost as fast as me on that

thing."

One side of his mouth quirked as he flipped the phone to face her. But it wasn't just amusement. It was something lighter, easier. His eyes lit, sparking with a boyish charm that softened the rugged edges of him, making him look like the kind of man who once grinned through wild adventures and ridiculous dares, who'd probably been trouble in his younger years but the kind you couldn't help but follow anyway.

Something about it was unfair. Because it made him approachable, disarming, and she wasn't prepared for that.

"They're wood yurts. Wood stove heating. Natural air conditioning—"

She arched a brow. "As in open the windows?"

Gabe waggled his eyebrows, leaning in slightly, just enough to steal a fraction of her breath. "You got it."

Her fingers tightened on the edge of her desk, a fleeting pressure to steady herself. Too aware of the space between them.

"The beds are in the loft," he continued, his voice low, easy, like this conversation belonged only to them. "Sleeper sofa, as soon as we buy those, in the living room."

He held the phone for her, the warmth of his hand close enough that she could feel it, even if they didn't touch. She swiped through the pictures.

The next one caught her attention.

A gangly boy, bright smile, full of something Gabe carried in his own expressions, and his mother. Her straight back and the fine lines of her face made it clear she'd walked through tough seasons and come out stronger. Snow covered the landscape behind them, the blue-hued mountains fading into the sky like something permanent, resilient, just like them.

Gabe chuckled, a quiet, deep sound that curled around her unexpectedly. "That's my sister Haydon and her son Harlan."

"When was it taken?" Renata asked, this time with a softness she hadn't expected to feel.

She wasn't asking just to make conversation. She truly wanted to know, especially after seeing the light in Gabe's eyes as he spoke about them.

"January, I think. First day back to school after break. Haydon is a bit sappy about those things. Even though she'll never admit it."

Renata's heart warmed, feeling a little closer to him. To his family.

"She looks strong. Confident."

"She is."

The pride in his voice wove through her like a lariat, tugging her a little closer. She leaned toward him slightly, but Gabe didn't move back. Didn't retreat.

"Yurts."

He chuckled. A deep, low sound, knowing. Like he recognized what she was doing.

"Yurts? Still?"

She tucked her lower lip between her teeth, fighting the urge to laugh too.

"They aren't accessible, right?"

He hissed air through his teeth. "Unfortunately, not the yurts. We have a few accessible rooms on the ground floor of the lodge."

"Already finished?"

He shook his head. The movement was slow, deliberate. "I mean, the construction is mostly done. Just need furniture and decor."

They chatted for another hour, Gabe filling in details, leaning in when he talked, lowering his voice when he explained things, as if every word was meant only for her.

At some point, she stopped trying to ignore his thrilling presence. Stopped pretending she didn't feel it. She just hoped he didn't notice.

But then, too late, she looked up. And Gabe was watching her. Still. Steady. Seeing.

She swallowed. But it did nothing to steady her. His unreadable gaze lingered, making her doubt that he hadn't noticed at all.

5

THE WOODEN PORCH creaked beneath Gabe's boots as he settled into the worn rocking chair, the rhythmic back-and-forth easing the tension he hadn't realized had gathered in his shoulders. The scent of sun-warmed earth hung thick in the air, and dust carried lazily on the evening breeze, settling into the quiet like it belonged there.

The sun dipped low behind Dalton Peak, casting deep shadows on the side facing the bunkhouse. The funny little Arizona mountain seemed out of place against the vast open desert. Nothing compared to the scale and breadth of the Swan, Mission, or Salish Mountains back home. Just one lone peak. A few more brownish looking ones in the distance.

The sun blazed bright orange and deep reds against what had been blue sky a few moments ago. Just like Montana sunsets had a way of stretching a man thin, Arizona's had the same pull. Nudging thoughts into places they didn't belong, places he didn't want to go.

Montana's dusks faded into cool, crisp twilight, long shadows stretching over endless hills and pine-lined ridges. Arizona's bled into fire, igniting the sky in streaks of copper and gold, burning red against the rugged desert.

It was beauty in contrast. Like it shouldn't work, but it did.

Different mountains made by the same God. Probably

with the same purpose. Like forcing a stubborn cowboy sitting on a ranch porch to think about a woman who made him question things he'd rather leave alone.

Gabe shifted in his chair as his younger brother handed him a lemonade. Ross plopped down on the other rocker with a heavy sigh.

"No matter how much I miss Montana, Arizona has kinda grown on me," Ross said, leaning back, boots kicked up onto the railing. "Not sure I see myself leaving."

"Oh?" Gabe's brow lifted. His brother's comment surprised him.

"Settled into life. Used to the summer heat."

"After three years, probably should be."

Ross snorted. "Might come up for the summer, though, when the busy season ends. Not much to do around here. Even though the Vargases let some of us stay in the bunkhouse, the paychecks are light or non-existent if they don't have some renovation projects planned. Like this year."

Gabe grunted. "I'm sure Haydon and Harlan would love to see you again."

Ross chuckled. "But not my big brother?"

"Seeing you now. Might be sick of you by then."

Ross's laughter faded as he angled his head toward Gabe, watching him in that way younger brothers did when they were onto something.

Gabe felt his collar tighten.

"You've been real quiet lately," Ross said, stretching his arms over his head before settling in deeper.

Gabe exhaled, rolling his neck once, then twice. "Been busy."

Ross snorted. "Busy staring into space?"

Gabe shot him a look.

Ross grinned, too amused for his own good. "Just saying, you've been distracted, and unless the bunkhouse walls are whispering sweet words to you at night, I'm guessing it's got something to do with a pretty resort manager."

Gabe's jaw ticked.

Not answering was still answering, and Ross was too perceptive to let it go.

Finally, Gabe shrugged, gaze fixed on the distant horizon where the sky burned against the desert like an ember refusing to die.

"She's got enough on her plate. The guy left her to raise a kid alone."

It came out flat. A deflection more than a real answer.

Ross hummed, rocking forward slightly, arms resting on his knees. "That so?"

Gabe kept his eyes trained forward. As if heat hadn't climbed up his neck. Or his heart bucked like a bronco at the mere mention of her.

Ross huffed out a quiet laugh. "You say it like it's just a fact. Like it doesn't mean anything to you."

Gabe ignored the way his chest tightened and his pulse raced. He huffed, gripping his lemonade tighter, the condensation slick against his palm. "Doesn't matter. Not my business."

But even as the words left his mouth, the thought sat heavy. Unshakable.

Ross let the silence sit between them, like he was waiting for the truth to settle in first.

"Too much like Haydon," Gabe grumbled.

Ross shifted slightly, considering. "You sure about that?"

The words hit Gabe sideways. His fingers tightened on the armrest of his chair.

Ross rocked back again, easy, but his eyes flicked toward Gabe, piercing and knowing.

"Heard something," Ross continued, voice measured. "Over at the dining hall the other night."

Gabe stayed silent. Waiting. Not sure he wanted to hear whatever came next.

Ross didn't make him wait long.

"Word is, she's not keeping the kid."

Gabe's eyebrows furrowed. Just barely. Not enough to be obvious. But enough for Ross to notice.

A quiet beat stretched, the weight of the words sinking in, settling somewhere deep, somewhere Gabe didn't want to acknowledge.

She'd be a good mother.

He knew it deep in his gut like he knew how to breathe air. Had seen it. The quiet, protective way she carried herself. The way she already cradled her belly without thinking. The way she softened, just barely, just enough, when she thought no one was looking.

This didn't fit. None of it did.

"You okay there, brother?" Ross asked, voice edged with something close to amusement.

Gabe exhaled slow. "Just thinking."

Ross laughed, full and easy. "Yeah, that's the problem."

He wasn't wrong.

Thinking got him into a heap of trouble. Like a half-built guest ranch he didn't know how to finish or run. Or like feelings boiling inside of him about the dark-haired beauty. The very pregnant one. Who was going to give up her kid?

He shook his head. Still wasn't buying it.

Ross stood and stretched, groaning loudly. Then he squeezed Gabe's shoulder.

"You know it's okay for you to have feelings for her, right? She's single. Sure, maybe there're a few complications in her life—"

Gabe snorted. "Mine too."

Ross expelled a loud breath. "You know, I might not be an expert on love—"

"Whoa! Hold up. Who said anything about love?"

"Me. I did. As I was saying, I might not be an expert. But watching a few of the Vargases and Adan Franco fall in love, fall hard, seems to me there's no perfect time for it."

Gabe leaned back, his grip tightening slightly on the

armrest. Love. The word wasn't supposed to be part of this. Wasn't supposed to fit into whatever was brewing in his mind.

Ross angled a knowing look at him. "Just saying... Who are we to argue with God's timing?"

A surprising surge of pride filled Gabe. Ross sounded downright spiritually mature just then.

Didn't mean God was pushing Gabe toward love, though.

He watched his brother disappear into the bunkhouse, but the thoughts Ross planted stayed put.

Still wasn't buying it.

But now he wasn't sure if he was trying to convince Ross. Or himself.

RENATA SCRAPED HER long hair into a clip as she ran the water until it warmed, then measured a dollop of face wash onto her hand. Raina-approved, organic, chemical-free.

Not her favorite. But it did the job.

She splashed the warm water on her face and dabbed it dry, flicking off the bathroom light. The house was too quiet. Terri was still in California, which meant no familiar footsteps down the hall, no idle chatter pulling Renata out of her own head.

No distractions.

She crossed the room, her heartbeat drumming a few beats too fast. Something felt... off.

Not alarming. Just off.

With a hand resting lightly on her belly, she eased onto the edge of the bed and kicked off her flip-flops.

The ache started dull. Low and steady, barely more than an afterthought.

She shifted, shaking it off as fatigue, maybe dehydration,

until the second wave tightened through her abdomen. Sharper, more defined than before.

Not normal. Or maybe it was.

She hadn't tracked every milestone, hadn't nested, hadn't let herself think too far ahead. This part of the process was meant to come and go. Quickly, cleanly, without complication.

Still three weeks before her due date. It was too early, right?

Three weeks. Did that matter? Did she need to call Mom? Did she need to do anything at all?

Another clench, slow but firm. Like her body was testing itself, practicing for something inevitable.

She should know more than she did. Should have paid better attention.

Maybe she was overthinking it. Could be nothing. Could pass in an hour, maybe two. If she just waited, if she ignored the slow tightening long enough, maybe it wouldn't turn into anything.

The thought settled for half a second. Enough to make her hesitate.

Then another wave crested, sharper now, gripping tight before easing again.

Her fingers traced slow circles over her belly, the instinct automatic, but the weight of it sat heavier than before.

She hadn't planned for this part. The wondering, the waiting, the uncertainty.

Was this how Raina would feel? If things had been different?

Would she be sitting in her own dim bedroom, running her hands over the same curve, feeling the same slow, tentative waves of something inevitable? Would she already know what each tightening meant? The baby's movements, the body's silent signals, the way motherhood settled into the bones before the child was even born?

Maybe Raina would have been excited. She'd planned

for this, waited for this. But Renata wasn't meant to linger in the moment.

Had she missed something? Had she miscalculated what real contractions felt like?

Hadn't Madison, her cousin Derin's wife, gone through some early contractions before Maverick was born? What were they called?

Her pulse ticked unevenly as another tightness rippled through her abdomen, stronger now, more insistent. She needed to do something.

Renata fumbled for her phone, hands too tight, too fast, unlocking it on the second try.

Braxton Hicks? It had to be. What if it wasn't?

Her water hadn't broken, so it shouldn't mean anything.

But her throat constricted as another pain rippled through her abdomen, sharp enough to steal her breath for half a second.

Not unbearable. But worse than before.

She should have read more, asked more questions, memorized every tiny sign that could mean something was wrong.

She needed to breathe. To distract herself. To do anything except sit here alone in the silence, waiting for it to pass.

Her fingers hovered over her phone screen.

Gabe.

She hesitated. Why him?

She could call Raina. Could call Devon. They were Cliff's parents. She was carrying their one hope for a biological child.

But she knew exactly how that call would go.

Raina would hear the strain in her voice before she even finished her sentence. Her concern would spike fast, all-consuming. Devon would tell her to go in right away, maybe insist he would call ahead and meet her there with Raina.

That wasn't necessary. Not yet. This was probably nothing.

But the answer came just as quickly as the doubt.

Gabe wouldn't hover. Wouldn't panic. Wouldn't make it more than it needed to be.

Another tightness rippled through her abdomen, sharper this time, lingering just a second too long. She sucked in a slow breath, pressing a hand lightly against her belly, waiting for the discomfort to fade. It did, but not fully.

Her pulse ticked unevenly as she stared at the phone screen, hovering. She could call Raina. Could call Devon. Could do what she was supposed to do.

But then it would turn into a flurry of instructions. A panic she wasn't ready for. A call she would regret.

Gabe was the simpler choice.

Maybe that was the reason. Maybe it wasn't.

Her fingers flexed around the phone, the cool glass smooth beneath her thumb, grounding her for a beat even as her thoughts scattered.

She could send the text. Could make this easy. Could let Gabe be the simple, practical choice.

But something about it didn't feel simple. He noticed things she didn't always mean to show. Saw hesitation she wasn't sure she wanted to acknowledge.

She didn't want to overthink it. Didn't want to let the moment stretch longer than necessary.

Her thumb hesitated for half a beat before tapping out the message.

You busy?

The little dots bounced while she waited for his reply.

Why?

Her breath came too fast, uneven. Her fingers hovered over the keyboard. Another slight wave pulled at her belly — not unbearable, but enough to solidify the decision.

Another wave tightened through her abdomen, insistent now. She straightened slightly, pressing her fingertips against her belly, waiting for the tension to pass. It didn't.

Not fully.

She typed before she could second-guess it.

Can you take me to the hospital?

6

GABE FROWNED AT the perplexing text.

Renata wanted him to take her to the hospital. Why him? Not her family? The place was swarming with them.

Maybe she felt embarrassed. Ashamed. Ross's words about her giving up the kid nagged at the back of his mind.

Then it hit him, hard, fast, like the kick of a spooked colt.

A jolt ran through him, sending heat rushing through his veins. His grip tightened on the phone, the smooth glass slick beneath his suddenly damp fingers.

She needed to go now. Not later. Now.

A sharp breath punched through his chest as he stabbed the call button, climbing behind the wheel of his truck.

"Where are you?"

Her voice crackled through the line, strained, carrying something beneath the surface.

"At home."

His stomach clenched. "Which is where?"

"The building across the way from the bunkhouse. I'm close enough to hear when the boys get rowdy."

He spotted two buildings, eyes scanning fast. "Which one?"

"I'll be on the front porch. Can't miss me."

He didn't waste another second.

Gabe punched the button to end the call. He shifted into Reverse, tires grinding against gravel. Then he jammed it into Drive. The cab felt too small, too warm, like his pulse alone was heating the air. His fingers flexed against the steering wheel, stiff with tension, the smooth leather damp beneath his grip.

Gravel popped under his tires, sharp and uneven, matching the erratic beat hammering inside his chest. He exhaled sharply, too fast, too tight, then rolled toward her place, parking his passenger door with easy access to the porch.

Then he saw her.

His gut tightened.

The porch light cast soft shadows across her face, but it couldn't hide the fear written in every tense line of her body. Her arms crossed tight, like she was holding herself together, her weight shifted subtly, like she wasn't sure she'd stand steady for much longer.

His stomach knotted tighter.

"Here."

Gabe swung the passenger door open, moving fast, wrapping an arm around her side as she leaned heavily into him. Her body was warm against his side, the subtle tremor in her frame making his hold instinctively firmer. Her breath hitched, a whisper of heat against his collarbone, barely audible but impossible to ignore.

She felt perfect against him. Right height. Not too short. Not taller than him.

His grip tightened just slightly — too aware of the way she fit, the way she felt solid but fragile at the same time.

He shoved the unbidden thoughts aside. Not the time.

"Here. Use the running board."

His hands braced her waist, warm against the curve of her body, lifting her gently as she reached for the grab bar, pushing up. For the first time in his life, he wished he had a lower vehicle. For her sake.

She settled into the seat, breathing unevenly, fingers gripping the door panel like she needed something steady.

Gabe shut the door firmly and rounded his truck, his boots hitting the gravel harder than they should.

He hopped into his seat and pulled away fast, gravel and dust kicking as his tires spun.

"Left or right?"

"Left. Here. Give me your phone."

He handed it over, heartbeat still ticking too fast, and soon navigation instructions came over the speakers.

"You should arrive at your destination in twenty-six minutes."

His throat constricted, and he pounded a fist against his chest, his voice rougher than he meant for it to be.

"You gonna be okay? Not gonna have this kid in my truck, are you?"

Her breath hitched. "I don't know! I've never given birth before!"

That landed harder than he expected.

Renata didn't sound calm. Didn't sound put together, prepared. She sounded small. Frustrated. Like she was trying to grip control and losing it at the same time.

Gabe forced himself to calm down. Not an easy feat. But she needed him with a level head.

He glanced at her briefly. Her fingers were tight against the edge of the seat, breathing shallow.

Why hadn't she called her family?

His grip tightened on the wheel, knuckles paling beneath the strain. He didn't understand it. Didn't like it. He hated not understanding it.

The question hovered on the tip of his tongue. Not the time.

"It's too early."

The panic in her voice nearly undid him. And confused him.

If she was giving up the kid, why did she care so much?

A sharp pulse shot through his chest, tightening his grip on the wheel. His arms locked, rigid, fingers pressing deep into the leather-wrapped steering wheel as the thought settled.

His gaze flicked to the directions on his phone. Twenty-five minutes. No turns for several miles.

He pressed harder against the accelerator.

Should he pray with her? Talk to her?

Twenty-three minutes.

He held out his hand on the console, fingers wiggling.

"Rennie."

Oops.

He'd heard her sister use the nickname, but he had no right to use it. Even though he liked the way it rolled off his tongue.

"Renata. Give me your hand."

A beat. Then two.

Then her soft fingers curled around his rough ones. He loosely gripped it.

"Any pain now?"

His voice was shockingly calm, a stark contrast to his rising anxiety.

"No."

"Good. Did you happen to time the contractions?"

"It was two in the matter of maybe ten minutes. Then nothing."

Gabe didn't know if human birthing worked like cattle or not. But God had designed both processes. And if Renata wasn't having close contractions at regular intervals, she was probably fine.

Not that he really knew.

Twenty-one minutes. He nudged the speed another notch higher.

He was so in over his head.

"Thanks."

The word hung heavy in the air.

"I just… My family… It's complicated."

He didn't like that answer. Didn't like the way her voice

carried something she wasn't saying outright.

"None of my business."

Though he was so curious, he could barely stem the dozens of questions in his mind.

Like why she felt she couldn't call them? Like why him? Like why give up the baby when she would be an amazing mom?

The thought slammed into his chest as a brief image of her holding a little black-haired baby in her arms floated through his mind. He pictured himself in the scene. Her looking up at him with that something more that had been flashing in her eyes for a few days whenever he caught her staring at him.

It felt... Homey. Welcoming.

Made him ache to the center of his being with longing for that.

Just that. Not her.

Lie.

Her. And the baby?

Gabe stifled a groan. He'd let Ross get in his head.

"Turn left now."

The navigation startled him from his thoughts.

A few minutes later, he pulled under a portico, rounded his truck, and helped her from it. He left her side only long enough to park in a visitor's space.

Panic sliced through him when he didn't find her right away.

"She's just down the hall. Third door on the right," a nurse instructed him.

Gabe jogged toward the room, heart slamming against his rib cage—until he spotted her in the bed. Talking to the doctor.

The tension in her face eased, causing the tension in his muscles to do the same.

After a few minutes, she waved him over to her bedside.

"They think it's false labor. Braxton Hicks contractions."

Relief hit hard, rushing through him so fast it left him lightheaded. For a brief moment, he didn't move—just felt the weight of everything, thick in his chest. Gabe swiped his hat from his head, gripping the brim tightly as if the pressure could ground him. He raked his fingers through his hair, exhaling sharply, forcing the adrenaline out of his system.

"That's good, right?"

She nodded, a small smile curving up the corners of her mouth.

"They want to keep me for a while longer. Check the baby's health."

Her eyes misted. Darted to the corner of the room. A slow blink. A quick swallow. The kind of quiet grief that didn't spill over, but was there, just beneath the surface.

His throat constricted, feeling her heartache deep in his gut. It settled there, heavy, unshakable. Never experienced anything like it.

And that's when Gabe realized he was in deep. Too deep.

And there wasn't a single part of him that wanted to climb out.

The thought lodged itself in his chest, thick, immovable. Like the kind of truth a man couldn't shake even if he tried. Even though he should.

THE MORNING AIR carried the scent of fresh coffee and the sweetness of blooming desert wildflowers as Renata stepped into the resort office, forcing steadiness into her movements, even though her body wasn't fully cooperating. She needed today to feel normal.

Emails to answer, staff rotations to finalize, VIP arrivals to oversee. Her cousin Derin had sent a request last night to confirm the casitas were properly stocked for his professional athletes arriving to rehab at the Sports Complex. Nothing she hadn't handled before.

But the weight in her chest hadn't left her since last night. And ignoring it was becoming impossible.

She pressed a hand absently against the desk, breathing through the lingering tension as she settled into her chair. The resort was waking up. The hum of conversation carried from the dining hall through her open window. Boots scuffed against the epoxied floors. The rhythmic clatter of mugs met tables.

Then Gabe. His voice drifted in, casual, grounding, frustratingly familiar.

He stepped inside a moment later, hat in hand, looking far too comfortable in a space she hadn't expected to be hyper-aware of him in.

"Morning."

She nodded, fingers tightening around her pen. "Morning."

Silence stretched just long enough to be noticed.

Then Ross's voice cut in from the front desk. "Hey, Gabe, how was the hospital run?"

Renata's stomach dropped too fast, too hard. The air stilled, tight, suffocating, as silence pressed between them.

Gabe's jaw flexed as his gaze flickered toward Ross, unreadable but firm. Without hesitation, he turned on his booted heel, crossing the lobby in a few long strides, dragging his brother toward the exit with a muttered comment Renata didn't catch.

Renata hurried behind him, only to stop short at the sight of Raina. Gabe. Ross. Solana. But her sister wasn't looking at them. She was looking at her. And the weight of that gaze nearly knocked the breath from her lungs.

Renata's gaze darted to Cliff's mother. Raina's expression wavered, hurt flickering across her features, too raw to mask.

Ross muttered something under his breath, quick, sheepish, before tipping his hat and ducking toward the exit. Leaving behind a silence thick with unanswered questions.

Renata felt exposed.

"Hospital?" Raina's voice was measured. Too measured.

Renata forced herself to straighten, pressing her fingers too firmly into the front desk counter. "I handled it." Her pulse stammered against the words.

Raina's gaze shadowed. Searched hers. Dissecting. "Handled it? And you didn't tell me?"

A slow coil of pressure tightened at the base of Renata's throat. She glanced at Gabe, not certain what she hoped for. A steady feeling just by looking at him? It hadn't helped.

He stayed quiet. Stoic. Watching. Taking in the exchange with a look that said he knew something was off — but not enough to piece it together. Maybe that was for the best. She didn't have the energy to explain Raina's interest in her pregnancy.

She turned back to Raina, exhaling harder than necessary, shifting slightly, trying to shake the tension creeping through her shoulders. The argument that had been on the tip of her tongue for months slipped free. "You don't have to hover."

"That's not the point." Raina's words landed too fast, carrying something closer to hurt than frustration.

Renata held her breath. She didn't want to hurt Raina. But she didn't want to be scrutinized right now, either. Especially not in front of Gabe.

"It's not just about you, Renata." The words hit hard. And shame followed, sharp and undeniable.

She knew how much Raina longed for the entire pregnancy experience. Cravings. Feeling the baby kick inside her. And, yes, hospital visits. These reasons, and more, were why Renata had agreed to be her surrogate. She regretted that her secrecy hurt Raina. Hated it.

Gabe's gaze flickered at that, barely, but she saw it. A

crease of confusion, quiet but telling.

Solana shifted slightly, crossing her arms, but didn't say a word. Like she was waiting. Watching. Weighing if she should step in. Perhaps praying.

Renata pressed her lips together, pushing back the regret and fear threatening to take hold. Desperate to escape.

Raina let out a slow breath, shaking her head before turning and walking out, shoulders slumped forward, head hung low.

Renata barely breathed as she ducked into the safe confines of her office, shutting the door behind her like it could hold back everything pressing in on her. The confrontation with Raina still vibrated through her, an unease she couldn't shake.

She collapsed into her chair. Picked up her pen. Forced her mind into work mode. Focus. That's what she needed. Casitas to check. VIP accommodations to finalize. Schedules to confirm. Tangible, manageable details — things that didn't require her to untangle emotions she had no business feeling. Not today.

The scent of coffee drifted in through the open window, mingling with the warmth of the desert breeze. And for a moment, she let herself breathe it in. Pretend she wasn't still reeling. From the encounter with Raina. From last night. From the hospital. From the way Gabe's voice had anchored her in the middle of something terrifying.

It had been too easy to trust his steadiness. Too easy to let him carry some of the weight, to curl her fingers around his for even a second of relief. She couldn't afford that kind of reliance. Couldn't afford the way her heart quickened every time he entered a room.

Then the door swung open, and the handsome cowboy stepped inside, silver-blue eyes full of compassion. He had a way of moving like he belonged anywhere he chose, calm and deliberate, like nothing rattled him. His gaze settled on her, lingering for half a second longer than normal. The exhaustion. The effort. The way she was pushing through like nothing had happened.

"You okay?"

Her fingers tightened around the paper, and she forced a small smile. "Just getting some work done."

"You know you don't have to handle everything alone."

The pulse in her throat kicked up. The weight in her chest deepened. But then he kept talking.

"Giving a child up for adoption is noble, though. Good. Right."

The room shrank instantly. The air thickened, pressing against her ribs. Her stomach turned sharply, the weight of his words landing somewhere far too deep, far too exposed. Her pen hit the desk, forgotten.

For a moment, she didn't move. Didn't breathe. Just felt it settle. Thick. Suffocating.

Then — abrupt and sharp — she turned to him. "You don't know what you're talking about."

Renata stood too fast, grabbed her keys, and escaped before anything else could unravel inside her. The golf cart's engine hummed to life beneath her as she swung into the seat, pressed down on the accelerator, and tore out toward the Sedona Casita.

Away from him. Away from everything she had almost let herself feel.

7

GABE WATCHED THE dust trail kicked up behind her golf cart, disappearing faster than she had any right to. A muscle in his jaw tightened.

She was good at running. Not just now, but always dodging, deflecting, slipping past him with well-crafted avoidance tactics. And the worst part? He let her.

He'd thought, for a moment, that he might finally get her to say something real. About her baby. About her plans. Instead, he'd struck a nerve. And she had shut him out so fast he still felt the residual force of it vibrating through him.

His fingers curled around the brim of his hat as he exhaled slowly, trying to shake off the frustration winding tight in his chest. He had two choices. Go after her. Or pack up and go home.

Both were equally extreme. Both were foolish in their own ways. Neither one would get him anywhere.

He was halfway convinced he should start packing, anyway. Montana felt far less complicated right now. Leaving would be clean. Simple. No messy conversations. No digging into things that weren't his business. No trying to figure out why Renata kept shutting him out. Or why she acted like she didn't feel this thing simmering between them.

And she wouldn't stop him. That much he knew. He could walk out today, pack up, drive home, and she wouldn't chase after him. The thought sat heavy in his chest, pressing deeper than it should have.

But instead of heading toward the bunkhouse to start shoving things into a duffle, he walked back to the office, sank into his chair, and picked up the pile of planning notes Renata had organized for him with a precision he hadn't even asked for.

The ink was crisp, purposeful, the handwriting clean though one or two notes looked hastily scribbled, as if she'd written them in a rush, balancing too much at once. He picked up a page, the corner slightly bent, catching the faintest trace of her warm, floral perfume.

She had done so much. More than he'd expected. More than he'd deserved.

The urge to return the favor gnawed at him, not just in a practical way, but in a way that left something unsettled in his chest. It wasn't just about gratitude. It was about wanting to do something for her, to make things easier, to understand her in a way that didn't feel possible through the layers of silence she had thrown between them.

Before he could wrestle with it any further, his phone vibrated against the desk. Haydon.

Gabe hesitated before answering, rolling his shoulders, guarding himself against any bad news. "Hey."

His older sister's voice came through clear, familiar, steady in a way Gabe needed right then. "Checking in. You still alive?" Haydon sounded amused, which meant Ross hadn't spilled everything to her yet.

"For now."

Haydon let out a low chuckle. "Things going alright?"

Gabe rubbed his jaw, weighing his words. "They're moving forward."

Not a lie. But nowhere near the full truth.

Haydon hummed knowingly. "You sound like you'd rather be back home."

Gabe almost agreed. Almost said yes, almost let the frustration spill out. But then his gaze landed back on Renata's notes. And something inside him twisted.

"She's been helping," he admitted, surprising himself.

"Renata?"

Gabe frowned slightly. Had Haydon been expecting that answer?

"She knows what she's doing," he muttered, flipping one of the pages over, scanning a list of vendors she had personally called for him. "She set up details I wouldn't have figured out for another month."

Silence stretched between them for a second too long. Then Haydon sighed.

"She's got a lot going on."

Gabe narrowed his eyes at that. "How do you know?"

Another pause. Then Haydon let out a breath, and her voice dropped just slightly, as if she was aware Harlan or a ranch hand might overhear.

"You remember how I felt before Harlan was born?"

Gabe stiffened. She wasn't talking about motherhood in general. She was talking about the prospect of having a child without a husband to back her up. About Vern not agreeing to her crazy marriage of convenience until a few months after Harlan was born.

He barely swallowed, the realization pressing into him before he could shake it off.

Haydon continued, voice quiet, measured, loaded with something close to understanding. "She's handling it. In her own way. But maybe you don't push too hard."

Gabe sat back, staring at the wall, his mind circling the pieces. Haydon had barely said anything. And yet everything felt heavier. Like he understood just a little more. Like he didn't want to understand the rest.

He forced himself to exhale. "Alright."

Haydon didn't push further, just changed the subject to ranch updates before they wrapped up the call.

Gabe set his phone down, staring at the notes a moment longer before finally standing, dragging himself toward the dining hall.

He'd seen glimpses of something more in Renata before. Just moments, barely long enough to notice before she hid them away. Like the way her mouth had curved just slightly at something Ross had said in the dining hall last week, only for the smile to vanish as soon as she caught herself. Or the time she had almost told him something real, her voice softening, hesitation flickering, but then the wall had slammed right back into place.

He thumbed the edge of one page, the ink crisp, the details thorough. The effort was there undeniable. And yet, she still held so much back.

Now, staring at her notes, he wondered how much of herself she held back not just from him, but from everyone. And why it bothered him so much.

He rolled his shoulders, stretching out the tension, but it stayed lodged somewhere deep. Nagging. Insistent.

He needed food. Needed a distraction. Needed to sit in a room full of people and feel normal again.

Yet, the moment he stepped inside, he felt the space working against him. The hum of voices layered over the clinking of silverware, over the occasional burst of laughter from cowboys fresh off the pastures. The smell of grilled steak mixed with the warm scent of baked bread and something cinnamon-heavy from the dessert trays near the far end of the room.

Normally, this was grounding. Normally, the routine of it settled him. Tonight, it just made him feel more alone.

He found an empty table near the wide, folding glass walls, left open to erase the barrier between indoors and out. A soft breeze drifted in, carrying the scent of rose blossoms, the refreshing spring air filtering through the space like it belonged. It should have bolstered him. Instead, it pressed against him like something he couldn't escape.

Gabe rolled his shoulders, stretching his neck, but the stiffness refused to leave. He pushed his fork idly against the steak in front of him, appetite dulled, jaw tight.

Renata's absence was irritatingly obvious. And that was a problem.

Because he shouldn't be this affected by her. Shouldn't be this preoccupied with trying to figure out why she kept holding back. Shouldn't be sitting here, surrounded by conversation and familiarity, yet completely detached from all of it.

Her walls had become his walls, and he wasn't sure when that happened. Or what it meant.

He pushed at his steak with the side of his knife, not really interested in eating, barely paying attention to the passing comments between tables. Then he caught something.

A voice, lowered but distinct, carrying across the dining hall from a small group of wait staff near the kitchen entrance.

"Seriously, if Renata hadn't stepped in, I don't know what I would have done."

Gabe stilled. His attention sharpened before he could stop it.

Another younger voice, grateful, threaded with something close to relief. "She said it was nothing, but she fought for me. I didn't even know HR could do that."

A pause, then a soft laugh. "Now, I get full-time hours with benefits starting next week."

The group exchanged quiet murmurs of agreement, appreciation passing between them, the tone one Gabe recognized well, the way people talked about someone who had done something good without asking for recognition.

He shifted in his chair, staring at his plate, stomach tightening.

Renata wasn't just good at her job, she was good to people. And the funny thing was, she wouldn't even think twice about it. She'd probably dismiss it outright if he mentioned it.

Which made it worse. Because how could someone so

deeply ingrained in the lives around her still act like she couldn't lean on them? Let him carry.

She had secrets. Burdens she refused to let others carry. Let him carry.

He wanted to know why. And he couldn't admit why it was so important to him.

THE QUIET INSIDE her home felt heavier than usual, settling over her like a weight she couldn't shift. Renata wasn't ready for it, not really, but she had convinced herself she needed it. That solitude was the answer tonight.

Silence had always been easy for her. Routine. A way to reset when emotions ran too high. But this wasn't silence. Not really. This avoidance stretched over the walls of her home like something tangible.

It wasn't just quiet. It was too still, pressing into the walls, settling into the seams of her home like something that refused to leave. Even her own breath felt too loud, breaking against the silence like an intrusion.

She curled her fingers around the warm ceramic of her mug, watching the dim glow of ranch lights beyond the property through the kitchen window. The tea was untouched, cooling against her palms. The events of the day pressed into her chest, leaving her restless, uncertain, teetering on the edge of something she wasn't ready to name.

Then a knock.

Her pulse ticked up, her fingers flexing against the ceramic mug before she set it down, carefully, deliberately, as if giving herself a second to steady. The knock came again, soft, patient, unwavering.

She exhaled before moving toward the door, already knowing who it was. Solana.

Her sister stepped inside without hesitation, moving

with the kind of familiarity that came with years of understanding each other without words. But tonight, Solana's gaze wasn't casual. It was measured, searching, carrying the kind of concern that came from knowing when Renata was holding too much back.

"You didn't call me."

Not angry. Not demanding. Just the truth. A truth laid out plainly, leaving little room for deflection.

Renata stepped aside, letting her in, because there was no point in pretending this conversation wasn't going to happen. "I was fine."

Solana exhaled, arms crossing loosely as she watched her carefully. "You called Gabe."

Renata stiffened. The name landed heavier than she expected, pressing into the space between them like something she couldn't push aside.

Her inhale was too shallow, barely steadying her pulse as she turned toward the kitchen, busying herself with her mug—as if rinsing it out might wash away the tension spilling into the room. She hadn't expected Solana to say his name so quickly, hadn't prepared for the way it would land like an unspoken question.

Solana followed slowly, deliberately.

"You live five minutes away, Rennie."

Renata tightened her grip on the porcelain. She knew. She had known exactly how close Solana was when she sent that text to Gabe instead. Knew she could have reached out. That help had been right there. But the truth was more tangled than she wanted to admit.

She swallowed hard, setting the mug down, fingers smoothing against the countertop, grounding herself in the motion before finally speaking. "I didn't want to take you away from Adan and Jet."

Solana's expression softened, but carried something unresolved in her eyes. "You think I wouldn't have come?"

Renata looked away. "You're a newlywed with a stepson." Her voice felt thinner than usual. "I didn't want to pull you from it."

Solana took a slow step forward, uncrossing her arms, voice steady. "You wouldn't have been pulling me from anything."

Renata inhaled slowly, trying to ease the tension building in her chest, but it wouldn't settle. "It wasn't just that."

She had meant to leave it there, to let that be enough of an answer. But Solana just stood quietly, waiting, giving her space but not retreating. The kind of patience only someone who knew her deeply could offer.

And maybe that was why, after a beat, she finally admitted, "I was afraid you'd say something to Raina or Devon."

Solana's gaze flickered, disappointment settling there, though she didn't voice it outright. "I never would, Rennie."

And Renata knew that. Of course she did. Solana had kept her secrets before, had stood beside her, protected her when things were hard. But this wasn't just a secret. This was everything.

She had trusted Gabe to keep quiet. Knew, without a doubt, that he wouldn't tell Raina, wouldn't mention a word to Devon. She had been desperate to keep them from worrying. Or hovering.

But Solana? It wasn't about trust. It was about fear.

Because if she let Solana in, if she gave voice to all the complex emotions churning inside of her, she risked falling apart completely. And that was terrifying.

Should she take the chance and tell her?

Renata turned, bracing her palms against the countertop, pressing harder than necessary, as if that alone might keep her steady. Her breath shuddered.

Then her hand hovered over her abdomen, hesitant, uncertain. Her fingers curled slightly, pressing just enough to feel the faintest resistance, the warmth of life moving beneath her touch. The connection was undeniable, terrifying, something she hadn't let herself acknowledge fully until now.

"I love him."

The confession was so soft she almost didn't recognize it as her own. Her fingers pressed lightly against her stomach, the touch instinctive, unsure. This baby wasn't hers. And yet the ache inside her said otherwise.

Solana didn't react immediately. She just reached out, fingertips grazing Renata's wrist, offering reassurance. "I know."

Renata exhaled, uneven, shaky. "I don't know how I'm going to give him up."

Solana's grip tightened, not in force, but in comfort. "You don't have to rush through processing this."

Renata pressed harder into the countertop, closing her eyes briefly.

"You don't have to work yourself into exhaustion just to avoid thinking about it."

She barely swallowed, her throat tight.

Solana's voice dropped slightly, careful, deliberate. "After the baby arrives, take time."

Renata shook her head, not in disagreement but in resistance. "I have responsibilities."

Solana exhaled, patient but firm. "You need to take care of yourself. You've sacrificed the last nine months for Raina and Devon."

A pause. "And Cliff."

Renata's eyes moistened.

Then Solana's tone softened, carrying the kind of warmth Renata wasn't ready for, but needed. "Even if it's just a few weeks away. Even if it's a trip, do something for yourself. Take a break from sacrificing for everyone else and give yourself time to heal."

The words settled heavily in the space between them. Renata wasn't sure how to respond.

She had built her life around giving to others, solving problems, keeping things running. Never stepping back long enough to ask what she needed. But what did she need? She didn't know anymore.

Solana didn't push further. She just let the words sit. For the first time in a long time, Renata let them.

A slow breath pushed past her lips, uneven, shaky. She hadn't realized how tight her chest had been—hadn't realized how deeply she had braced herself against the possibility of feeling this much. She let her fingers relax against the counter, the warmth beneath her touch steady, grounding.

Maybe Solana was right. Maybe she needed to do something. Take a step. Let herself start figuring out what came next—before the decision was made for her.

Her fingers curled around the soft fabric of her dress, as if gripping onto something unseen. Then, without a word, she nodded.

Not an agreement. Not yet. But maybe a first step toward considering her future.

The weight of it settled, pressing into her chest, not heavy, but present. And for the first time, the thought slipped in, quiet, but sure.

Maybe this had been God's plan all along. Maybe, just maybe, she was finally ready to take the first step.

8

THE OFFICE WAS too quiet. Not in a peaceful way, not in the way silence should bring clarity. This kind of quiet felt crowded, heavy, thick with thoughts she had been shoving aside all week.

Renata shifted slightly in her chair, rolling one shoulder, then the other, trying to ease the tightness creeping in. She had felt off all morning, unsettled in a way that had nothing to do with work and everything to do with the slow-building pressure twisting through her stomach.

Her fingers skimmed against the edge of the table absentmindedly, the notes in front of her blurred beneath the weight of everything sitting behind her ribs.

Life after Cliff's birth was almost here. She couldn't bear the thought of sitting at Sunday supper week after week, watching Cliff gurgle happily in Devon's arms. Pretending it didn't hurt when she saw Raina tuck a blanket around his tiny body, leaning into the kind of warmth Renata had tried so hard not to want for herself.

How, if she stayed, she would have to see it all, again and again, until her heart either hardened or broke completely. And she wasn't sure which one scared her more.

A slow ache rippled deep in her abdomen, sharper than before. She inhaled carefully, pressing the palm of her hand against her belly, waiting for it to pass.

It did. Mostly.

She knew, distantly, that she should pay more attention to the way she felt, should track the waves of discomfort with something closer to caution. But the thoughts in her mind drowned out everything else.

Like what to do after Cliff arrived. When he met his parents, and was no longer her responsibility.

She wasn't sure when Montana had started to feel like an answer. Only that it had begun settling into the spaces left by uncertainty, pressing in like something steady, a contrast to the storm brewing inside her.

Maybe when she saw that picture of Haydon and Harlan, standing against those beautiful peaks, the sky stretched wide around them, crisp, endless, and open.

A few days of that. Just a few. Maybe a week. Or a little longer.

How refreshing would it be to gaze at something untouched, quiet, far from everything familiar?

The thought settled deep, heavier than she wanted it to. She pressed her fingers gently against her wrist, as if anchoring herself, but the pull toward open skies and quiet peaks had already taken root.

A moment from her first interaction with Gabe came to mind. His reaction when he first found out she was pregnant. He had expected six weeks of her time, six weeks of mentoring, and she had known from the beginning she wouldn't be able to give him over four.

That was before she realized just how much help he needed.

Just imagine what she could do if she were onsite. Decorating the yurts—a smile stretched across her lips, remembering how the funny name had almost become a joke between them. She could find decor that matched the surrounding land, choosing colors and textures that made the space feel less temporary, more intentional.

She could meet Haydon and Harlan.

Her smile tightened and fled when another wave of

something beneath her ribs tightened, shifting, making her inhale just a little sharper.

She could do even more for Gabe if she went to…

"I've been thinking about Montana."

Gabe barely lifted his gaze. "Montana?"

She pushed forward, her voice smoother than it should have been, steadier than she felt. "Helping you. After the baby."

That got his attention.

His head came up fully this time, his brows knitting together, silver-blue eyes locking on her in undisguised confusion. "What?"

The stunned way he looked at her made her regret saying anything at all. But she couldn't take it back now.

She met his gaze, willing herself not to falter. "After the baby arrives, I could come up for a while. Help you settle things at the ranch."

He stared, blinking once, slowly, like he was trying to force his brain to catch up. "Renata, we never…"

Gabe straightened, his face impassive. But his voice was laced with suspicion when he spoke. "We talked about me staying here for a few weeks. Not you leaving."

Her fingers tightened against her belly, and she sucked in a sharp breath, waiting for the pain to fade. "I've been thinking about it."

Thinking about Montana. Thinking about leaving the resort. Her family's ranch. Her hometown. Her life.

The way he stared at her told her everything she needed to know. He wasn't just confused. He was shocked. Thrown off course.

And for once, she wasn't avoiding it. She was watching it play out, watching the way he processed it, watching the way it hit like something he didn't have the tools to unpack.

His voice dropped slightly lower, rougher. "You'd take a newborn across the country?"

Her stomach twisted sharply. She hadn't expected that

question so quickly, or maybe she had, but hated that he asked it.

She inhaled sharply, gaze darting away. "I wouldn't be taking him anywhere."

Silence.

Gabe's frown deepened, his jaw tightening as if something about that didn't sit right. "You wouldn't—?"

Renata felt a sudden sharp wave of pain tearing through her, stealing all the air from her lungs.

A contraction.

Her breath came uneven now, her pulse ticking up just slightly. It was the second one. The first had been minutes ago, passing just faintly enough that she dismissed it.

This one was different.

She was going into labor.

The realization slammed into her, stealing whatever breath she had left. This wasn't just happening. It was happening now.

Cliff would be here soon.

And after this—after she placed him in Raina's arms, after the weight she'd carried for nine months was no longer hers, after her heart would be ripped from her chest. What would be left?

Where would she belong? Where would she even go?

Could Montana be the answer?

MONTANA. RENATA WAS talking about Montana. Helping him.

The words landed like a punch to the gut, knocking the wind out of Gabe before he could catch his footing. She was talking about Montana, his land, his ranch, his future. And for the first time, he realized he wanted her there. Not just as some helpful guide, some mentor who had been slowly shaping his plans from a distance. He didn't want to be apart from her. Not now. Not in ways he hadn't even admitted to himself until this very second, sitting across from her, watching her tell him she was considering leaving everything behind to go to Montana. After the baby.

Gabe stared at her, his brain stuck between two opposing thoughts. Ross's offhand comment weeks ago and the very real fact that Renata was sitting in front of him, saying words that didn't make sense. She wasn't keeping the kid. Ross had said it like it was a fact, like it was something Gabe should already know. And Gabe had accepted it, let it sit in the back of his mind, left it alone because it wasn't his business.

But now she was talking about Montana like it was some perfectly reasonable, logical next step, and Gabe couldn't see how any of it connected. She'd take a newborn across the country? No. That wasn't what she said. She said she wouldn't be taking him anywhere. His chest tightened as he tried to make sense of it, tried to work through the pieces like they could somehow form a full picture if he looked hard enough.

"You wouldn't?"

Renata shifted, the smallest adjustment in her seat, but something about it felt off. Her fingers dug into the table briefly, then lifted, pressing against her belly like she was grounding herself against something invisible.

Gabe frowned. "You alright?"

She swallowed. "Fine."

Liar. She wasn't fine. Something about the way she was sitting, breathing, moving was just slightly off, like she had started adjusting to discomfort before she even consciously acknowledged it.

Then her breath hitched, sharp and sudden. Gabe stood before he could think about it.

"Renata."

She blinked rapidly, inhaled too carefully, fingers pressing harder against her stomach. And then her body tensed. Something locked up inside her, tightening, pressing, stretching. His pulse kicked up. That wasn't exhaustion. That wasn't stress. That was something else. Something serious. Something immediate.

A contraction.

His stomach tightened violently as she exhaled, uneven, a crease forming between her brows. This wasn't the first one. The realization settled like lead in his chest. She'd had at least one before this. Had ignored it. Had convinced herself it wasn't happening. Until now.

"Renata." His voice was sharp now, urgent. "You're in labor."

She opened her mouth to argue, to deny, to force him to back down, but then another contraction hit her. And this time, she couldn't argue at all.

Gabe didn't hesitate. "Let's go."

He was moving before she could protest, his hands hovering but not pushing, giving her just enough space to find her balance as she stood. Her jaw tightened, her breath uneven, but she let him guide her toward the exit, toward the truck, toward the reality she had been refusing to face.

The moment they stepped into the lobby, Solana turned in her chair, her gaze catching instantly on Renata's expression. Gabe barely slowed down as he passed her.

"She's in labor," he tossed over his shoulder.

Solana stiffened, but Gabe didn't stop to explain. Didn't wait for her reaction. In a blur he barely registered, he helped Renata into his truck, kinda grateful for the trial run a week ago. Kinda not.

He was her what? Friend? Cowboy she was mentoring in business? He didn't know what he was. A calming presence. He could be that. He should be bothered by the whole thing. Only met her a few weeks ago.

Climbing behind the wheel, he pointed his truck toward the hospital. That he knew how to get to because that would be something an expectant father would know. Gabe tried to shove the bizarre, yet appealing thought from his mind. Drive. Focus. Get Renata there safely.

And then they were there.

The waiting room buzzed with controlled urgency, nurses moving between stations, voices murmuring in soft tones about patient updates. Gabe had barely settled Renata into a chair before the intake nurse caught sight of them, eyes sweeping across the scene before landing on him with easy assumption.

"Dad?"

The single word slammed into his chest, knocking the wind out of him before he could brace for it. His body went rigid, not from anger, not from embarrassment, but from something deeper, something too reckless to name outright.

Renata froze, fingers gripping the armrest, her breathing uneven, like she wasn't sure if she should correct the nurse or let Gabe do it himself. Gabe didn't react fast enough. Didn't correct her. Didn't say no. Because for half a second, just one wild, fleeting second, he realized he might be okay with that. That assumption. That role. That place beside her in this moment.

The thought punched through him so hard, so violently, that he almost stood just to shake it off. Renata turned her head toward him, her gaze flickering with an almost apology, but not quite. Like she knew this would happen. Like she had braced herself for it but hadn't prepared for how it would make him feel.

His jaw tightened, muscles tensing before he finally forced out the correction. "I'm not—"

Renata's sharp exhale cut through him, her body pressing back into the chair as another contraction hit. Everything moved too fast after that. A nurse called someone over. Someone else was checking Renata's pulse, firing off questions Gabe barely heard. Then the rush. The wheelchair. The corridor. The transition into the delivery room swiftly, pushing Gabe into motion before he could think, before he could plan, before he could figure out what he was supposed to do.

He was supposed to leave, wasn't he? Step aside? This wasn't his place.

But then Renata reached for him. Not dramatically. Not desperately. Just without thinking. Fingers curling into the fabric of his sleeve, holding onto him for half a second before she let go. And that was enough. Enough to keep him in the room. Enough to make him stay, even as everything inside him spun further out of control.

Like the father-to-be. But not.

The thought shouldn't have hit him as hard as it did. But it did. It landed like something he hadn't allowed himself to consider until now, something buried too deep to name, too impossible to admit. Weeks of watching Renata's hands settle against her belly, protective, instinctive. Weeks of catching glimpses of emotions she wouldn't voice, ones he didn't dare ask about. Weeks of looking at her and, heaven help him, secretly wanting this baby to become his. Which meant he wanting something with her too.

Until now. Until the second she reached for him, not because she needed him, not because she was afraid, but because he was here. Because he had stayed. His pulse slammed against his ribs.

They hooked Renata up to monitors. Told her to push. Her screams ripped through him, twisting everything inside him in ways that shouldn't have been his to feel. Helplessness clawed at his ribs. He hated seeing her in pain. He hated feeling helpless, unable to ease her burden. And that scared him more than everything else.

And then Devon appeared first. Then Raina.

And everything shattered.

Raina's voice cut through the chaos, loaded with relief, sharp with concern, too much emotion packed into every syllable as she rushed toward Renata, ignoring everything else in the room. Ignoring him.

"You're here. I didn't know you were already in labor. We were on our way."

Renata reached for Raina, and Gabe's brain short-circuited. Rebooting. Nothing made sense. Not. A. Thing.

A nurse turned toward Raina, smiling, guiding her closer. "Here, Mama. Let's get you ready to hold your baby."

Gabe's stomach dropped so forcefully he had to tense his legs to stay standing. The blood drained from his face.

And then "She's a surrogate."

The words slammed into him like a wrecking ball, splintering everything. Renata wasn't the baby's mother. The baby wasn't hers. He wasn't hers to keep. She was never Gabe's to hold. And he hadn't seen it. Hadn't understood it. Hadn't known until it was too late.

Renata exhaled sharply. Barely a shift, barely a sound, but something about it wrecked him. She wasn't just letting go. She was preparing for it. Doing what she had to do. Because she had no choice. No. Choice.

His chest tightened, his pulse hammering, his balance nearly failing. He had been a fool. A dreamer. A man stupid enough to let himself want something that was never his to want. He had let himself imagine, just for a second, just for one impossible, fleeting moment, that this child, that Renata, could have been his life. That maybe when she reached for him, it had meant something more. That maybe God had lined up just enough pieces for him to step into something meant to last. That maybe, just maybe, God had given him a family.

But God hadn't given him anything. Not this. Not her. Not a child that wasn't his to keep.

And just like that, the dream disintegrated. Gone before he ever had the chance to hold it. Before he even understood what he wanted.

And now she wanted to leave. Not just to put distance between herself and what she was losing. But because staying meant breaking. And breaking wasn't an option.

Go to Montana. With him. To…

The realization landed like a sledgehammer to his ribs. She needed escape. Because giving the baby to his rightful parents would destroy her. Gabe had seen her heart, serving others to the point of exhaustion. But this was beyond sacrifice. This was loss.

And suddenly, a different truth crashed into him. This wasn't about him. It never was. It was about her. It had always been about her. And if he couldn't save himself, he could save her.

Gabe would take her to Montana. Give her a purpose. Help her find healing. Even if it cost his heart everything. Even if God alone knew if it would be enough.

9

―――――

FIVE DAYS.

Renata downed an ibuprofen, pressing the pill bottle harder into the counter than necessary before forcing herself to move. Her doctor assured her the pain would subside soon. It was normal after giving birth and not breastfeeding. Well, her doctor had said it differently, using words like choosing not to nurse and mother. Which she was not. Had never been.

For the rest of her life, she would mark one more pregnancy on the ObGyn paperwork than whatever number of children she had. If she had children. If she could climb out of this emotional crater of grief.

She had to get out of here. Out of Arizona. Away from text messages from her sister, her mother, her cousins' wives, and her aunt. If one more Vargas stopped by or texted or called, she thought she might just lose it.

Renata turned off notifications from the family group texts and photo shares. She couldn't. She just couldn't look at the pictures of Cliff. Tears poured down her cheeks in quiet streams. She didn't try to stop them anymore. Didn't fight it. She let it come whenever the emotions, or hormones, pressed too deep.

She pulled a suitcase from the closet, tossing it onto the bed with more force than necessary. It sat there empty, waiting, inevitable. She inhaled too sharply. Exhaled slower. Felt something in her chest tighten before she shoved it down, shoved it back, shoved it anywhere except where it could reach her.

Her movements felt noticeable, deliberate, like she had to concentrate on every task. Yet somehow, she felt detached, as if she were watching a movie about herself but not really in it. She folded dresses, jeans, loose-fitted t-shirts, placing them carefully on one side. Too carefully. Each movement slow, deliberate, too controlled, like if she packed too fast, she might not be able to stop herself from breaking apart.

Her fingers hovered for half a second over a sweater she wasn't sure she'd need. She dropped it in anyway. Closed the drawer too hard. She zipped the suitcase, her grip too tight on the fabric, her pulse uneven as she pulled the metal track shut. And that's when she noticed her hands were trembling.

She stared at them, at the way her fingers shook against the edge of the zipper. For just a moment, she let herself feel it—feel what she was doing, feel what she was leaving behind. Then she shoved it down. She had to.

She grabbed her jacket, swung it over her arm, plopped her cowgirl hat on her head, and tore herself away from the weight of feeling like a mother but not being one.

As she dropped her suitcase wheels onto the floor, a slip of yellow fabric fell to the ground. A fresh wave of soul-ripping grief crashed over her. She ought to leave it behind. Ought to throw it out. But she couldn't. It was her one connection to the son that wasn't hers. To Cliff.

A cute onesie she'd bought with cartoon-like bunnies. It had made her smile that day in her second trimester. She intended to give it to the baby as a gift. Now she couldn't part with it. Needed something to soothe the raw ache in her soul.

Gabe was waiting. She heard his truck rumbling outside. She needed to go. Holding the onesie to her cheek, she rubbed the soft fabric there as if it could absorb some of her pain, her loss.

A knock came from the door. Renata moved slowly, tucking the yellow keepsake into the bottom of her backpack style purse. She couldn't leave it behind, even if she left him behind. Her fingers wrapped around the cold metal of the doorknob to her home. She glanced over her shoulder one last time, spotting that stupid lumpy couch. How many movies and pints of ice cream had she shared with her sister from the couch?

Then it hit her. She wondered when—if—she would return.

"Ready?"

Gabe's gentle voice nearly undid her again. His warm hand rested on her shoulder. Renata couldn't keep it together for one second longer. She collapsed against his sturdy frame, taking comfort in sharing a small part of her burden with him. His arms wrapped around her warmly, as if his touch could infuse life into her again.

It couldn't.

Since the delivery, she'd only felt comfort and compassion from the man. No judgement. No criticism. Deep, profound respect. And sensitive care beyond measure. His hand rested lightly over her head—something that reminded her of her dad, yet not. Something more. Something she didn't have the energy to name. But something she desperately needed.

Renata dug into the last of her reserves, pushing herself hard to straighten her back and raise her chin. It was time to go. Without fanfare. Without a send off. Like a thief in the night, but not.

Montana wasn't just waiting. It was pulling her forward like something inevitable, like something more than just a place to go. Like somewhere she might finally learn how to live with the break inside her. And Renata had to be someone else now. Not because she wanted to be. Because the person she had been before Cliff, before all of this, was already gone.

GABE'S GUT ACHED at the sight of her. Or maybe his heart ached. Or both. He couldn't tell which.

The dark circles under her eyes stole the warmth from her face, the glint he'd seen when she had teased him about yurts long gone. Now, her eyes looked hollow, stripped of light, stripped of joy. She was adrift, unmoored, like a buoy tossed into open waters, barely tethered to anything.

Lord, help me to be that anchor for her. Help her to find You through this season.

Gabe grabbed the handle of her suitcase, slinging her computer bag over his shoulder. Then he reached for her hand. It was limp in his, her fingers slack, unresponsive, like she hadn't even noticed him holding onto her. Gabe curled his fingers loosely around hers, rubbing his thumb over her knuckles, offering warmth, steadiness, support. She didn't grip back. Didn't react. Just let him lead her toward his truck, following without resistance, without real awareness, without energy to do much else.

He stowed her luggage in the storage bin of the horse trailer next to his, his chest tightening when he saw the feminine floral pattern beside his duffle. It felt normal. Like it belonged there. And yet not.

Gabe tucked her laptop bag behind the seat, pausing for half a second, half-hoping she might say something, half-knowing she wouldn't. Renata had already scrambled into the passenger seat, dropping her purse backpack thing between her feet. Tossing her hat in the narrow space behind the seat. She curled into place without adjusting, without moving, just folding into it, like she needed to disappear.

Gabe climbed behind the wheel, exhaling slowly. Sent

another prayer heavenward. For safe travels. For her. For whatever lay ahead of them in Montana.

She stared out the window. Not moving. Not blinking. She wasn't seeing the landscape—they both knew that. She was just letting herself be lost. The truck rumbled beneath them, tires cutting smoothly across the open road, stretching toward Montana like it had a purpose stronger than either of them could name.

And still Renata didn't say a word. She sat stiffly in the passenger seat, face turned toward the window, but not really looking. Just existing in the silence.

Gabe kept his hands loose on the wheel, glancing her way every so often, waiting for some signal that she wanted to engage. It didn't come. The quiet pressed in, the kind that felt unnatural, not the peaceful kind of quiet, but the kind that made everything too heavy, too thick, too suffocating.

He cleared his throat, throwing a light, easy question. "You wanna pick where we stop for lunch?"

No reaction. Not even a flicker in her expression.

He tried again. "We're passing through some towns with solid BBQ, but don't I know if you like BBQ, so I'm thinking, you call it."

A pause. She shifted slightly, picking at the sleeve of her shirt. That was it. Nothing more.

Gabe exhaled slowly, adjusting his grip on the wheel. Alright. Talking wasn't gonna do it. Time for desperate road trip measures.

He leaned back, keeping his tone casual, teasing, easy. "Alright. Road trip game. Classic 'Would You Rather.' You ready?"

Still nothing. He pushed forward anyway. "Would you rather fight one horse-sized duck or a hundred duck-sized horses?"

Silence. He sighed. Then a breath. Not his. Hers. A small one, barely noticeable, but it wasn't heavy or forced. It was sharp, surprised. Like she hadn't meant to react at all.

Then her head tilted, just slightly. Still stiff. Still hesitant. But he saw the movement. Saw her register the absurdity of the question, even if she didn't respond. Saw the hint of something lighter trying to fight its way through.

She murmured. Not loud, not clear, but just enough for him to catch it. "That's ridiculous."

Gabe grinned, fighting the urge to push further. She had spoken. It wasn't much. But it was something.

He nodded, letting the game drop, letting the silence sit for just a little longer before shifting the conversation. "My dad always told us Montana was about more than land. Said it wasn't just where you lived—it was something you carried. A responsibility. A way of life."

Renata's head tilted again, just a fraction more than before. Not much. But enough.

Gabe kept going. "He drilled it into us growing up, my sister, me, and Ross, that we weren't just inheriting acreage, we were inheriting something bigger. The grit, the work, the stubbornness it takes to hold on to it. It's what we're trying to pass down to Haydon's son now."

Renata shifted slightly, as if settling into the seat for the first time. Not much. But enough.

Gabe kept going. "Rolling pastures, wide open sky. It's always been home, but it took me a while to see beyond that. To see why my family held on to it for four generations. Why they fought for it. Why every winter, every drought, every hard season never made them leave."

And then she answered. Awkward. A little slow. Like she wasn't sure if she was allowed to engage. "I saw pictures."

Her voice was quiet, words almost swallowed by the hum of the truck, but they were there.

Gabe nodded, keeping his tone steady, easy. "Yeah? What did you think?"

Renata hesitated, exhaling slowly, her palm smoothing against her thigh. Then a shift. A flicker of something close to engagement. "I remember thinking it looked open. Like nowhere else."

Renata's fingers tightened against her lap. Not much. But enough. "Wide. Endless."

"Like a place you didn't just visit, but stayed."

And Gabe felt something settle inside him. Just a little. Just enough. Like proof that she was still in there. Still Renata. Even beneath the grief.

But just as fast, she caught herself. Her posture pulled inward again, her face turning back toward the window. Like she had let herself step too far forward, and now she needed to retreat again.

Gabe didn't fight it. Didn't push. She wasn't ready. But Montana was waiting. And Gabe was bringing her there. To his ranch. To his home. To his family. Not just because it was what she wanted. But because leaving her behind wasn't something he could do.

Maybe when they reached it, she wouldn't have to fight so hard to keep herself together anymore. And maybe he wouldn't either.

RENATA STIRRED, NECK stiff and sore. She must have fallen asleep. Gabe let her.

She blinked, disoriented, the unfamiliar landscape blurring together in the fading afternoon light. A freeway sign came into focus. Hoover Dam, miles ahead.

She should ask Gabe to stop. Stretch their legs. Explore the tourist stop. Take pictures. Except she didn't want any pictures of this trip. Of her life. Without Cliff. No evidence of her postpartum self with baby weight clinging to her bones, a body that still felt like it was supposed to hold him, a body that had prepared for him only to be left with nothing. No reminders of what she didn't have. What she would never have.

"Hey, want to stop at the Dam?"

Gabe's voice was gentle, offering, careful. Renata turned her face toward the window, hiding the tears slipping past her eyelids.

He kept talking, filling the space. "I stopped on the way down, so I took pictures to share with Haydon and Harlan. But if you've never been..."

She hadn't. And she wouldn't. Not this trip. Not like this. Maybe someday, in some distant future, where the new version of herself could feel something close to interest. Eagerness and excitement seemed too distant and too far out of reach. Just interest. It was the most she could hope for.

"Renata?"

His voice was so careful. So patient. She sniffed, wiped her fingertips over her damp cheeks, forcing herself to answer, even if it wasn't real, even if it was just words.

"No, thanks."

She heard his sigh, quiet, barely there, the kind that held helplessness more than frustration. She wished she could find the energy to feel regret for making his return trip home so difficult. She couldn't.

"You can sleep more, if that helps."

Renata leaned back against the seat, adjusting just enough to press deeper into the cushion, as if the fabric itself could absorb her exhaustion. She closed her eyes.

Praying for some kind of respite from anything that could lift her from this valley of darkness. Not to feel better. Not yet. Just to breathe. Just to exist, until something like Montana, time, or God could teach her how to do more than just survive. Could show her how to be Renata again.

10

THEY HAD BEEN driving down a private road for a while, the truck's tires rolling over packed gravel, quieter now, more sure of its direction.

Renata straightened in the seat, her spine aching from too many hours leaning against the window, muscles tight from holding herself in the same position for too long. The cold seeped through the glass, pressing against her skin, sharper than the dry Arizona winter. She was grateful for the winter coat Gabe had insisted she buy, though she hadn't thought much of it at the time. Now, feeling the chill settle against the closed truck window, she realized just how different this place was how far from home she had come.

She wasn't in Arizona anymore.

Gabe had said this was his ranch, the Broken Spur, according to the metal sign hanging over the entrance, dark letters stark against the evening sky, backlit by the last slivers of daylight slipping behind the mountains. The pastures stretched wide, open, unfamiliar, rolling in slow, quiet waves toward the horizon.

For the first time since they left, she felt something close to curiosity, an emotion faint but present. She studied the way the land moved, the way the wire fences divided sections of pasture, the way the ranch itself sat firm and rooted in the middle of it all. She forced herself to focus on the landscape, the sign, the curve of the road beneath the truck's tires. Not on the words "left home." Not on the ache that threatened to pull her under.

Her fingers pressed lightly against her lap as she unconsciously traced the letters of the metal sign in her mind, grasping for something steady before she could spiral again.

Then the ranch house came into view. Beautiful. Rustic. Rugged. Like the man next to her. The man who had made it his mission to show her extreme kindness, who carried a quiet understanding of grief in the way he looked at her, the way he never asked for more than she could give. She remembered him saying once that his parents had died suddenly, so he probably understood some of her grief. But some of it, he never could.

Renata sighed, studying the home. Larger than she expected, stretching wide with natural wood and stone, carrying a sense of solidness. It wasn't extravagant, but it was intentional, every detail meant to endure. Gorgeous picture windows framed the snow-capped mountains beyond, stretching endlessly across the horizon. A small covered porch shielded the front door from the elements. The grass closest to the house was more brilliant, still caught between green and yellow, like winter hadn't fully given up yet.

Gabe parked the truck on the concrete pad in front of the garage. Renata gathered her things, opened the door, and stepped out, the cold sinking past the thick fabric of her coat with an invigorating bite. The air smelled different here. Cooler, fresher, cleaner, threaded with the scent of earth and grass. Livestock. Wood smoke. The quiet hum of a place that carried work in its bones. It felt nothing like sunny, dusty Arizona.

Renata had barely adjusted to the chill when Haydon stepped onto the porch, her presence as steady as the land itself. She wore no coat but hugged her arms close against her middle. Her thick sweater probably warded off the worst of the chill.

She was beautiful without effort, practical, strong, Montana through and through. Her thick braid hung over one shoulder. No makeup, but the kind of confidence that didn't need it. Her boots pressed firmly into the earth, shoulders squared, a quiet kind of command in the way she moved.

Haydon's gaze flicked briefly from Gabe to Renata, holding there for half a beat, assessing, reading something neither of them said aloud. Understanding. Not pity. Not judgment. Just knowing.

She didn't hesitate. Didn't ask questions Renata wasn't ready to answer. She simply stepped forward and cupped Renata's hand in both of her warm, steady ones.

"I appreciate you coming. Really."

Her voice was low, even, carrying quiet gratitude, but no expectation. Renata felt the warmth of her hands, the quiet strength in them, and something in her chest loosened just a fraction.

Haydon gave her fingers the slightest squeeze before letting go, stepping back just enough to keep things easy. "Yurt's ready for you. Fire's going. Should be warm when you head in."

Renata exhaled, unsure if she was relieved or unsettled by how carefully Haydon seemed to read her. "Thank you," she murmured, forcing the words out even though her throat felt thick. The cold pricked the growing moisture in her eyes.

Haydon nodded. "Dinner's ready if you want it now. Otherwise, I can box it up. Whatever's easiest."

The kindness in that hit hard. No pressure. No expectation. Just options.

Renata's fingers tightened slightly around the strap of her backpack purse. She didn't know what she wanted. Didn't know if she could handle sitting at a dinner table, exchanging pleasantries like she wasn't dragging something unbearable behind her. But she did know one thing. Standing here in the cold with Haydon's quiet steadiness settling around her felt strangely safe. Maybe safer than anything had in days.

Gabe stepped closer, Harlan trailing behind him, the porch creaking softly beneath their weight. Haydon glanced back at Gabe. A flicker in her expression, like understanding, like confirmation that she saw what Renata couldn't yet see. She turned back to Renata, gesturing toward the door.

"Let's get you inside."

Renata followed her in, stepping across the threshold. The warmth met her instantly, wrapping around her, thick and steady, the scent of home-cooked food settling into the space like it had been waiting for them. Her mouth watered and for the first time in days, she wanted to eat.

Her boots clopped on the beautiful wooden floors, rich in color, the grain deep and natural, like they had seen years of footsteps, years of stories, years of weight. The ceilings stretched high above her, making the house feel expansive and open, yet somehow protective. Not just spacious, but deeply rooted, carrying the weight of years lived within its walls. It wasn't just a structure. It was history, a place that had borne the footsteps of generations and remained unshaken.

Then Gabe's touch. Warmth at the small of her back, light, steady. His voice, low, quiet, just for her. "I hope you like it."

A brush of his thumb against her coat, fleeting, unspoken. She wasn't ready to feel what was shifting inside her. But she felt it anyway. There was no avoiding it. Not the way his voice softened, not the way his hand stayed, not the way her own body registered the warmth before she could stop herself from noticing.

So she didn't say anything. Didn't acknowledge the tenderness of the moment, the intimacy buried beneath restraint. She shifted her stance instead, barely leaning toward him, toward the heat of his hand, toward the assurance of his touch. Not much. Just enough to let it be there. Just enough to feel it.

Gabe hesitated, just for a breath, just for the briefest pause in time, then his fingers moved to the front of her coat, gently holding the lapels open. "Let me get this for you."

His voice was low, easy, nothing heavy in the words. Even so, she felt it. Felt the brush of his hands as he helped her slide her arms free, the movement slow, yet carrying more significance than it should have. The warmth of his presence lingered even after the coat was gone.

She let him. Didn't argue. Didn't pull away. Just stood there, absorbing the quiet care, the way he made things easy without forcing them.

He draped the coat over one arm, then nodded toward the door. "I'll grab your things."

Renata inhaled, steadying herself, willing her thoughts to calm, to quiet, to stop focusing on the small things that felt bigger than they should. Gabe stepped outside after hanging her coat in the closet by the front door.

Haydon gestured toward the dining room, the scent of dinner wafting through the space. Warm, rich, familiar, the kind of meal that made a house feel like home. She glanced at Renata, reading something in her hesitation before offering a small, unspoken reassurance in her gaze.

"Come on in."

Just an invitation. It wasn't a push. Wasn't an expectation like it would have been with her family, well-intentioned or not.

Renata breathed deeply, held the moment for a second longer than necessary, then stepped forward. She had chosen to sit at this table tonight. And somehow that felt like more than she thought she had in her.

THE COLD HIT him harder when stepped back outside, sharp against the warmth still lingering in the house, the contrast unsettling in a way he couldn't quite name.

Gabe inhaled deeply, steadying himself, focusing on the rhythmic crunch of his boots against the frozen ground as he moved toward the truck. He hesitated for half a second before reaching for Renata's bag, the weight of the handle pressing into his palm, reminding him of the reality of this moment. She was here. In his home. Under his roof. And somehow that changed everything.

It began long before this. He'd watched her on the road trip, in the delivery room, fighting for pieces of herself she couldn't grasp, trying again and again to engage with the world outside her grief. And now here. Walking through his front door. Standing in the warmth of his house, absorbing his family, becoming a part of the landscape of his life, even for just a little while.

The feeling dug deep, sharp and unrelenting, catching him off guard in a way he hadn't expected. He wanted more. So much more. But she wasn't ready. And that was the part that held him back.

Haydon lingered in the doorway when he stepped back onto the porch, waiting. Watching. She tucked her arms around herself, the chill in the air catching the loose strands of hair that had come undone from her braid. She didn't say much. She never did when she was reading something in him.

But she glanced toward the dining room, toward where Renata was hesitating, fingers flexing slightly against the strap of her bag. Then Haydon's eyes flicked back to him. A knowing look. A quiet pause. Then her voice, low, even.

"She's beautiful."

Haydon gave him a look, something between understanding and confirmation. "I can see why you like her."

Gabe swallowed, barely nodding, his grip adjusting on the luggage before setting it down near the door. Haydon didn't press. Didn't push. Just left it there, left him there with his too-heavy thoughts, before slipping into the dining room, letting the hum of quiet conversation swallow her up.

She wasn't his. Maybe never would be. But she needed time, and for now, he would give her that. He shook off the thought as he hung his coat in the closet.

The house had never felt more whole than when family filled it, the warm hum of voices drifting through the open spaces, the rich scent of dinner filling the air. He watched Renata as he padded toward the dining room, so very aware of her presence in his home. The way she studied the space, lingering near the edge of the dining room like she wasn't quite sure where she fit.

Then a blur of movement. Harlan. The kid threw himself at Gabe, arms wrapping tight around his waist, face pressing against his sleeve like he'd been waiting all week for this moment.

"You're finally home!"

Gabe grinned, ruffling his nephew's hair, leaning into the hug with equal force. "Missed me, huh?"

Harlan stepped back. "Obviously."

Gabe laughed, shaking his head. "Well, I guess it's good to be missed."

Renata watched quietly, her expression unreadable but softer, something settling in her gaze that hadn't been there before. Then she turned toward Harlan, adjusting her stance slightly, testing the waters of conversation.

"What's school like?"

Harlan shrugged, unbothered, too focused on the fact that Gabe was home to put much thought into school. "Okay. I like recess."

Gabe snorted. "That's not an answer, kid."

Harlan ignored him, shifting his focus toward Renata instead. "But I like ranch stuff more. Way more."

Renata's brow lifted slightly. "Ranch stuff?"

Haydon moved around them, setting bowls onto the table, the warm scent of roast beef filling the space. Harlan grinned, eyes lighting up. "Like riding, helping with the horses, fixing fences. Last summer, I got to help with branding. I'll do it again this year."

Renata's fingers curled loosely against her lap, interest flickering through her expression. Seeing it lightened Gabe's heart. "You helped with all that?"

Harlan sat taller in his chair. "Yup."

Gabe smirked. "We wouldn't get anything done around here without him."

Harlan beamed at the praise, grabbing a roll from the basket before shoving half of it into his mouth.

"Grace first," Haydon warned.

Gabe took Renata's soft hand in his, pausing for a beat before taking his sister's. Then he bowed his head and thanked God for the safe travels and for the food and for home.

The hum of conversation settled into the room, easy, familiar, filling the space like it had always belonged there. For Gabe, everything about this place had always felt right. This house, this ranch, his family. But tonight, with Renata here, it felt different.

Haydon slid a dish of roasted vegetables toward him, nudging his elbow as she sat back in her chair. "Checked on your calf this morning."

He paused mid-bite, setting his fork down, giving her his full attention. "And?"

Haydon's lips tipped into something close to a smirk, but not quite. "She's doing fine. Starting to put on weight. Looks stronger."

"That new bottle regimen helped, then."

Haydon nodded. "Yeah. She took to it better than I expected. Good call."

He let out a slow breath, feeling the tension ease in his shoulders. Then Renata's voice. Soft. Curious. Like she was starting to step into this world, even if she wasn't sure she belonged in it yet.

"Bottle-fed calf?"

He nodded, choosing his words carefully. "Yeah. The heifer didn't make it, so we had to step in."

Renata's gaze flicked toward Haydon. "None of the other heifers would take her?"

"Nope," Haydon said after a beat. "First regimen was good for a few weeks. Then she seemed sluggish. So Gabe suggested changing up the formula. She'll make it now."

Renata nodded. She looked like she had more to ask. Like she was weighing how much she truly wanted to know about this place, these people, the rhythm Gabe had carved out for himself here. And he wanted her to see it. To feel it. To understand why it mattered. Wanted her to see that this ranch didn't just exist. It was lived in. It was held onto. It meant something.

Then Harlan cut in, leaning back against his chair, groaning while he stretched his arms over his head. "I'm ready for dessert."

Gabe snorted. "You barely finished dinner."

Harlan hitched his shoulder. "And now I'm ready for dessert."

Gabe snorted, shaking his head. Same old Harlan — dramatic, impatient, and entirely predictable. He hadn't realized how much he'd missed the chaotic rhythm of dinner, the easy familiarity, the way his nephew made everything feel like some grand event.

Haydon rolled her eyes, but amusement lit her gaze. "Fine. Go grab the cobbler."

Harlan shot out of his chair, disappearing toward the kitchen like it was the most urgent mission of his life. Gabe watched him go, a smirk tugging at the corner of his mouth. Kid never changed.

Then his eyes darted to Renata. She watched, and the corner of her lips twitching. Not quite a smile, but close. And that smallest shift, the tiniest ease in her expression — settled deep inside Gabe, blooming into hope.

Dinner wound down, laughter easing into low conversation, warmth lingering in the quiet hush of the evening. Gabe exhaled slowly, awareness settling deeper around him, the kind of calm that follows connection. He glanced toward Renata, who lingered near the doorway, watching, taking in the change. Maybe not the meal itself. Maybe the feeling of being here. Of belonging, even if she hadn't decided what that meant yet.

He helped her with her coat before shrugging into his own. Grabbing her bag, he nodded toward the door. "Come on. I'll take you over."

Outside, the air had dropped a few degrees, biting sharper against the edges of the night. The warmth of dinner slipped away, leaving behind a silence that carried more than just stillness. Renata pulled her coat tighter, her body angling slightly, her movements slow, as if adjusting not just to the cold but to being here. At his ranch. At his home.

Gabe opened the truck door for her, waiting until she eased into the seat before climbing behind the wheel. The drive to the yurt was short, but the silence between them ran deeper than the distance, unspoken thoughts pressing against the space they shared, words hovering just out of reach.

Renata stared out the window, watching the ranch fade into deep shadows beneath the wash of moonlight. She wasn't just looking. She was taking it in, weighing it, turning it over in her mind. And Gabe? He understood that. She wasn't shutting down. She wasn't retreating. Her presence was soaking into this place, into this life, not just passing through, but settling in.

The thought sent his heart soaring. But as the cold pressed in, as the night held them in its peaceful embrace, he realized he didn't want to let her go.

11

As Gabe drove toward the yurt, Renata's breath caught in her throat. The carriage light above the entrance cast a golden glow, spilling across the covered porch, chasing shadows from the wooden steps. It beckoned to her.

"Yurts."

The word slipped from her lips, unbidden. A remnant of her old self. A whisper of curiosity, something lighter, something untouched by grief. Gabe's chuckle filled the cab, warm and steady, wrapping around her heart like a comforting cocoon against the night's icy stillness.

She could do this. Montana would be good for her. New experiences. Meaningful work. Him. She barely registered the thought before she spoke again, voice quieter this time.

"It's more inviting than the pictures," she murmured. "We should get some photos of them, inside and out, for the website."

Gabe coughed a little as he shifted into Park. "Website... About that..."

She turned toward him, brow lifting slightly. "You don't have one?"

Talking about work, thinking about work, felt good. It gave her something solid to grasp.

"No."

Renata rolled her lips inward, considering. "My cousin's wife, River, put together one with a reservation system for the lodging association we belong to. I'll email her about it and get some rates if you'd like."

Gabe hesitated, just briefly, before nodding. "Yeah. Thanks."

The silence stretched between them, rich with unspoken meaning, neither of them rushing to break it. Then his throat cleared, his voice dipped lower, softer.

"I'm really glad you're here."

Renata ducked her head, fingertips grazing her knee, absorbing the words. How they lingered, how they made her pulse skitter, how they made her want to look at him longer than she should. It felt good to be here. With him. With his understanding.

"Looking forward to starting first thing tomorrow."

Gabe tilted his head slightly, eyes scanning her expression. "If you want to sleep in. Take a day. Whatever. that's fine."

"No." Her voice came out too quickly, tight around the edges, revealing more strain than she intended. "I'm ready."

He studied her for a beat longer, then exhaled, his voice laced with resignation. "Alright. Let's get you settled."

Gabe stepped out of the truck, rounded it, and opened the passenger door, offering his hand. She took it, fingers brushing his palm, absorbing the quiet strength he offered. He handed her the key, the cool metal pressing into her fingers as she stood at the bottom of the porch stairs, staring up at the wood-paneled entrance bathed in golden light.

She drew in a deep breath, the crisp air rushing through her lungs, cutting through the thickness in her chest. Peace wove through her, delicate but present, stretching into the spaces grief had hollowed out. She straightened her shoulders. Then she climbed the stairs, stepping forward, fully embracing this new season of her life, however long it lasted.

The door swung open, and warmth wrapped around her instantly, pressing against the cold clinging to her coat. The scent of wood, earth, firelight settled into the yurt. Stained pine everywhere. Maybe a little too much. A couch, some wall hangings, and a rug would make it feel more balanced, less like a structure, and more inviting. Renata could already envision pictures of Montana wildlife, color weaving through the monochrome tones of wood. If only her designer friend Cara lived closer. Then again, she could always call or text her for thoughts.

She glanced at the kitchen and stilled, surprised to find not just a full setup, but sleek appliances nestled against dark quartz, a striking contrast to all the pine. A small round table sat beside the curtainless window, framing the night sky. She imagined the view. Mountains stretching endlessly, just beyond the glass. She couldn't see them now, yet their presence was undeniable. The ranch house faced this direction. So did the yurt.

The connection between them, the ranch, the yurt, felt intentional, as if the Broken Spur was already working its way into her. A quiet pull toward the kind of peace that came from being surrounded by God's creation.

She was so engrossed in the space, in absorbing the foreignness of it, that she didn't hear Gabe snick the door shut behind him. His throat cleared, and she turned, catching the red warming his cheeks, the way he shifted his weight between his feet. Something passed between them, not awkwardness, not uncertainty, but something quieter. She didn't name it. Didn't acknowledge it. Just reached for the laptop bag.

"Here, let me have that. Would you mind taking the rest upstairs?"

Gabe gave a curt nod, handing it over before heading toward the loft. Renata tucked the bag onto the chair beside the small round table, fingers brushing against the wood backing, catching on the small carved opening of a black bear's silhouette. The rust-colored cushion beneath her palm was warm, soft, textured.

Gabe's voice drifted down from the loft. "Take off your

coat and stay a while."

A twitch of a smile pulled at the corner of her mouth, faint but real. She shrugged off her wool coat, hanging it by the door before toeing off her boots, the wood cool beneath her socked feet.

Gabe's footsteps sounded from the loft as he paused at the top of the spiral staircase, the elegant centerpiece of the yurt. "I was worried it might feel too cold up here."

Renata turned, tilting her head slightly. "But it's fine?"

"Yeah," he said, running a hand over the back of his neck, glancing toward the wood stove. "This little thing does a great job of warming the whole building."

And just like that, she let herself absorb the warmth, let herself breathe, let herself be here.

Renata crossed the room slowly, her socked feet pressing into the wood, the fire casting soft shadows along the walls, stretching gently across the space. Gabe descended the spiral staircase, his movements unhurried.

She knew he would leave. That had been the plan, the expectation, the way this night was supposed to end. But as he stepped closer to the door, something tightened inside her. The quiet would be too loud once he was gone. The silence would be too empty, too full of thoughts she wasn't ready to be left alone with. The memories waited. Lurking at the edges of her mind, pressing in, threatening to pull her under the moment, the strength of his presence faded.

Renata couldn't let him go. Not yet.

Her fingers flexed slightly before she spoke, her voice barely above a whisper. "Would you —" She swallowed, her pulse thrumming, the words fragile but real. "Would you hold me? Just for a minute."

The request hung between them, charging the air, pulling an invisible cord tighter around them. Gabe hesitated long enough for her to notice. Then he closed the distance between them, his arms wrapping around her with quiet certainty. Strong. Sure. Solid.

She leaned into him, her cheek resting against his chest, exhaling as the tension loosened in her shoulders, as the weight behind her eyes lifted just enough. His comfort wrapped around her, reliable and unshaken, pushing back the thoughts threatening to drag her under.

Then his fingers slipped into her hair. He stroked slowly, absently, letting strands slide through his fingers, letting the motion soothe the raw grief inside her. It was so small. So simple. But it calmed her. Anchored her, just for this moment, just for now. Kept her from slipping into the darkness again.

His voice was low, careful, meant only for her. "I've got you."

The words settled deep, like ripples fading across still water, like something quiet and certain beneath the surface. She closed her eyes, savoring the moment before opening them again.

Then he leaned back just slightly, meeting her gaze. His fingers brushed against her cheek, tucking a stray strand of hair behind her ear. A touch so fleeting, so careful, but enough to leave behind a sense of anticipation as soft waves spread through her.

His voice softened, barely above the crackle of the fire. "Get some rest, Renata."

A pause. Not rushed, not forced. "Lock up."

He stepped back. Then one last glance, one last hesitation before he murmured, quieter this time, "You can call me if you need anything."

And with that he was gone, the door clicking shut, leaving her in silence that carried too much. Renata pressed her palm lightly against her chest, as if the echo of his touch still lingered there. For just one more second, she let herself linger in it.

Then the silence crept in. Then the ghosts settled.

MORNING CAME TOO hard and too fast. Gabe had spent half the night chasing sleep that never settled. Now, with dawn stretching pale fingers over the ranch, he wrapped his hands around his coffee mug, letting the heat seep into his palms, grasping at routine. It wasn't working.

Because the moment he let himself drift, his body remembered. Her warmth, the quiet way she had leaned into him. And now she was here. She was on his ranch. Breathing the same cold air. Standing under the same sky. And he couldn't shake the way it changed things.

He tugged his beanie lower, shrugging into his coat with firm, deliberate movements, the morning air biting hard against his skin. Then, pushing away from the porch, he headed toward the barn, impressions from last night trailing him like an echo. But even as he moved forward, even as he tried to convince himself that this was just another morning, his thoughts kept circling back to her.

Was she warm enough? He'd made sure she had a coat before she arrived, insulated, suited for the wind. But now he wondered. Was she curled up in the yurt right now, tucking the blankets closer, adjusting to a cold that wasn't familiar? Had the wood-burning stove gone out? Did she know how to use it? He should have shown her last night.

The ground crunched beneath his boots as Gabe ambled toward the barn, a haze of breath swirling in front of him with each exhale. The ranch had always been his refuge, his rhythm the only thing that had ever stayed constant when everything else had turned upside down. Like when his parents died suddenly. Or when Vern passed away unexpectedly.

But now Renata was here. Just up the hill, in the yurt close enough to touch but just out of reach. And somehow, the land felt different. Like it wasn't just his anymore. Like she had woven into the fabric, the existence of this place, into the timber of his home, the spaces between each breath. Like she had altered him. Deeply. Irrevocably.

He wanted her here. Not just as a business partner. Not just as a guest. As Renata. The woman who had trusted him last night, enough to ask for comfort. The woman who, despite everything she had lost, had stepped onto his ranch into his world without hesitation. For herself. For him.

That realization marked a turning point he could no longer ignore. But it also meant something else. Meant she was stepping into a role Vern was supposed to fill.

Gabe exhaled deeply, shaking off the thought, rolling his shoulders as if he could push it loose. It wasn't the same. It wasn't fair to compare them. But Vern had been his buffer, handling marketing, reservations, logistics. All the pieces Gabe couldn't afford to overlook.

And now, there were only five weeks left until June. And he didn't even have a website. That fact sat like a weight in his gut, pressing hard, demanding an answer he didn't have. No website meant no reservations. No streamlined system for guests to book their stays. No easy way to secure income before the season started. Before the loan payments came due.

Vern would have had one built months ago, but Vern was gone. And Gabe had spent too long ignoring the problem, convincing himself he'd figure it out on his own. Now, Renata was offering solutions. She was the answer to prayers he had been to afraid to ask. Too proud to ask.

He needed help. That was the truth of it. But accepting hers meant admitting something bigger. That she was stepping into a space Vern should have filled. That Gabe's survival — the ranch's survival — might depend on her ability to pull this off.

Which made him uneasy. Not because he didn't trust her. But because trusting her meant giving up control. She had already lost so much, and here he was, letting her step into more responsibility, more pressure, more weight she hadn't asked for. Was he expecting too much? Putting too much faith in her?

The ranch was his responsibility. His burden. And yet, she knew what to do when he didn't. Her ideas flowed. Solutions came naturally to her. Renata saw paths forward when he was still stuck in the logistics, trapped in the mire of everything he hadn't figured out yet. If they opened on time, it would be because of her. And maybe that scared him more than anything.

Gabe sucked in a sharp breath, exhaling slowly. He needed to get out of his head. The scent of fresh hay and warm animal breath filled the barn as he stepped inside, reality pressing hard against his chest.

Haydon stood by the stall, hands in her coat pockets, watching the calf with a satisfied expression. "You worried for nothing," she said, nodding toward the calf standing firm on its legs, solid and thriving. "She's stronger than ever."

Relief hit fast, settling deep. A fleeting pause in the chaos. But before he could fully shake off the haze of his thoughts, Haydon caught the way his gaze flickered, just briefly, toward the stall window. Before he could stop himself, his eyes settled on the yurt, bathed in morning light. And for one split second, he could still feel Renata leaning against him. Feel the trust. Feel the warmth. Feel the quiet way she had worked herself into the foundation of everything he was trying to rebuild.

Then Haydon cut in, amused. "You're distracted."

Gabe huffed a breath, rubbing his fingers absently against the woodgrain. "I'm focused."

Haydon snorted. "Not on the calf."

She tipped her head toward the window. "She's got you thinking."

He wasn't discussing this. Clearly, Haydon didn't care.

"Must be nice having her up there, huh?"

Gabe exhaled, slow and measured, keeping his gaze firmly on the calf. "She's here to help."

"Mmm."

Silence stretched between them, heavy with unspoken meaning.

"You like her."

Gabe stiffened, jaw flexing. "Haydon —"

"Not saying you're in love."

The word hit his gut like a sucker punch, ringing far too close to the truth.

"Just saying you look at her like you want to figure her out. And men only do that when they care."

Gabe said nothing as the words settled into the tiny cracks in the walls around his heart. His sister had always read him. Too well. Haydon didn't push further. Just watched with practiced patience. Letting the words land.

Then she chuckled, patting the stall door. "Well, I won't say anything. But the next time you start pacing about her, maybe own up to what it means, huh?"

Gabe barely swallowed, staring at the calf as if it could provide an answer to the feelings churning in his soul. It couldn't. The truth? The more time he spent with Renata, the more he relied on her, the less secure he felt because it was his heart on the line. And that? That was dangerous.

He dragged a hand over his face, exhaled slowly, then rolled his shoulders, pushing off the tension as if he could shake it loose. It didn't work. His gaze moved from the barn doors across the wide stretch of ranch to the yurt. Her yurt.

Five weeks. Five weeks to figure out how to get the guest ranch off the ground, how to secure income, how to make this place survive. And somehow, she was already at the center of it.

Was she awake? Was she warm enough? He should check. He shouldn't check. Because needing her was one thing. But needing her this much? That was something else entirely.

Gabe pushed away from the stall, gripping the wooden beam at the entrance for half a second longer than necessary. Then, without another word, he stepped outside into the cold, into the silence, into a day already enmeshed with thoughts of her.

12

MORNING CAME SLOWLY. Not in the usual heavy, suffocating way, but in something softer. Something that didn't press down on her but simply existed, waiting, allowing her room to breathe. Renata stayed still for a while, buried beneath the blankets, her body snuggled deep into their plush warmth, the cool air pressing against her skin where her arm stretched past the edge of the covers.

She didn't move right away. Didn't force herself into wakefulness. Instead, she let the quiet settle. Let the stillness of the loft wrap around her, let the first hints of morning press delicately against the edges of her awareness. Her fingers curled slightly, the movement absent, more instinct than intention. Like some part of her remembered the security of another presence.

The realization crept in before she could stop it. Gabe. The feel of his chest solid beneath her cheek, powerful arms surrounding her, his tender touch careful in a way she hadn't expected. She hadn't thought much about what it would feel like to be held again. Not until she asked him. And when he did, it was without hesitation, without question. But it was also without assumption. She had felt it. The restraint, the deliberate respect of his touch. There had been no expectation in the way his hand rested against her back. Just presence. Certainty. Unspoken understanding.

Renata inhaled slowly, blinking against the soft morning

light filtering through the window. The memory hovered on the edge of her mind, more inviting and calming than she wanted to admit. She should get up. She should move. Because if she stayed here too long, letting her body remember too much, her losses would surface and destroy any sense of normalcy.

She pushed the blankets aside, stretching slowly, then padded toward the stairs. The cold bit at her bare feet, pulling her into wakefulness faster than she wanted. She descended the spiral staircase, gaze landing on the wood stove. The embers inside burning low, fragile, the heat fading faster than she expected. Her fingers flexed against the iron handle, then tightened around her phone as she turned away, tapping the screen to life.

She hesitated. Then, decisively, she sent Gabe a text. *Hey, can you show me how to work the wood stove?* Message sent. Done.

Renata moved fast now, pulling on her coat over her pajama pants, wrapping it tight around her shoulders to ward off the chill. While she waited for a response, she crossed the room to the fridge and opened it. It held more than she expected. Eggs, bacon, cheese. And tucked near the milk, a familiar bottle caught her eye. Hazelnut creamer. She hadn't asked for it, hadn't even thought about it, but Haydon had stocked it, anyway. How did she know? Gabe. Probably. The small gesture settled deeper than it should have. It made her feel cherished in a way she couldn't admit she needed. Should she thank him? Or Haydon? Or just enjoy their thoughtfulness.

She pulled the bottle out carefully, fingers tightening around the cool plastic, then reached for the coffee. Brewing. Pouring. Stirring the creamer in until the rich brown softened, steam spiraling toward her face. She inhaled. Closed her eyes. Let herself enjoy it. Just for a second.

Then, pushing forward, she moved to the stove, heating the skillet, pulling ingredients together. Eggs cracked against the bowl, bright yolks pooling, butter sizzling as it met the heat. Salt. Cheese. The rhythm steadied her. The simplicity and routine kept the dark thoughts at bay. She plated her breakfast and set it on the table before sitting in the chair facing the window, tucking her legs under her.

After praying for her meal, Renata ate while feasting her eyes on the stunning view of the snow-capped mountains. She had been right. She could see them from that window. Their towering, majestic presence calmed her. Seeped into her soul in a way that helped refresh her perspective. She set her fork down slowly, hands resting lightly against the edge of the table. A deep breath pressed into her chest, steady and full, the kind she hadn't taken in too long.

The quiet stretched, unbroken but tangible, pressing against the edges of the morning like a held breath. For the first time in longer than she wanted to admit, she let herself sit in the present. No urgency. No expectation. Just that restorative calm.

Boots thumped solidly against the porch, heavy and sure, cutting through the quiet like an inevitability. Renata stiffened. She hadn't fully thought through what it would feel like to have Gabe here inside the yurt, stepping into the morning before she was ready for it. And now, standing in her pajama pants, oversized coat, hair a tousled mess from sleep, she realized just how unprepared she actually was. Too late now.

With a deep breath, she pulled open the door. Warmth from the yurt clashed instantly against the crisp morning air. Gabe stood there, all fresh and masculine. Clean-shaven now, with early sunlight catching the edge of his jaw, casting sharp angles and soft shadows. His gaze lingered on her. Unreadable. But something in it made the heat on her neck crawl higher.

Renata stepped back, tightening her coat around her, wishing she had at least thrown on proper clothes. "In. Come... in." She cringed internally. What was that?

Gabe hesitated half a second. Maybe catching her awkwardness. But he stepped inside. His boots muffled against the wooden floor, the warmth of the yurt cocooning them both. The door clicked shut behind him. An ordinary movement, but somehow it made the space feel smaller. Tighter. Closer.

"Your feet!" Gabe's voice rumbled through her. "Put on slippers."

"Don't have any."

A deep V formed between his brows. "Socks. Boots. Something."

Renata stuffed her frozen bare feet into her boots before moving toward the stove a little too quickly, determined to salvage the interaction. "Uh—so, the fire..." She gestured vaguely, avoiding his eyes, suddenly very aware of how ridiculous everything was. Her lack of slippers. Her lack of knowledge about all things winter. Heat crept up her neck, not from the wood stove but from the sheer absurdity of how unprepared she felt. She couldn't even form a coherent sentence. Why did it suddenly feel like she'd forgotten how to talk?

"It's still burning, kind of, but the heat's not right. I didn't know how..." She exhaled sharply, pressing her lips together.

Gabe's eyebrows lifted. Amusement twitched at the corner of his mouth. "You need me to show you how to use the stove."

She nodded, refusing to meet his gaze. "Yeah. That."

Gabe exhaled slowly, turning toward the wood stove, fingers brushing the iron handle with easy familiarity. "You ever built a fire before?"

Renata swallowed, forcing herself to stop fidgeting with her sleeves. "Not exactly."

His gaze darted back to her. "Then I'll show you." His voice carried an assurance that made the space feel smaller, warmer, and more intimate. And Renata wasn't sure if that was because of the fire or because of him.

Renata tucked her hands into the folds of her coat, watching as Gabe crouched beside the stove, his movements unhurried, practiced, as if this process was second nature to him. He reached for the iron poker, shifting the embers slightly before laying a fresh log into the chamber. "Start small," he said, his voice calm. "Too much wood too fast suffocates the fire."

Renata nodded, watching the glow of the embers flicker beneath the added fuel. She should have known that. She stayed close as he struck the match and leaned in. The flames caught with a quiet crackle. Her knee barely brushed his as she moved, the warmth of the connection more noticeable than the fire itself. She stilled, fingers tightening slightly around the fabric of her coat, willing herself not to focus on it. Not to feel how near he was. She inhaled slowly. Warmth rising. Control returning.

"This helps," she murmured after a beat, nodding toward the stove. "Thanks."

Gabe straightened, glancing at her, but she didn't linger in the moment long enough to register whatever was in his eyes. Instead, she cleared her throat, shifting gears. "I got a quote from River for the website and reservation system," she said, hugging her arms around her middle. "If I put a rush on it, she can have it up in a week. But I'll need pictures."

It felt good to focus on the next steps. The reservation system, the website, making sure everything was lined up. Because that was what mattered. That was what she could control. Not the ache in her chest. Not the past. Just this — feeling useful. She inhaled deeply, swaying slightly on her feet before glancing toward Gabe, who had stepped back, gaze lingering on the mesmerizing flames.

"This is a good start," she murmured, motioning her open palm around the room. "But if we want welcoming, enticing photos for the website, I should probably furnish this place first."

Gabe didn't immediately respond, his posture tense, his thoughts clearly somewhere else. She pressed forward, already building the plan in her mind. "I'll need a few basics. Curtains, maybe a rug, a few pieces to make it feel lived in. It'll help sell the experience."

Gabe's nod was automatic, but Renata caught the hesitation in his stance, the way his weight shifted slightly as his mind was likely on everything else left undone. She exhaled slowly. "But I don't exactly have a way to get to town."

Gabe's gaze finally locked with hers, his eyebrows raising for a beat before settling again. He pushed a hand through his hair, exhaling softly. "I'll figure it out," he said simply.

Renata frowned. "I can help."

"Be back soon."

She nodded, watching him walk toward the door, his frame tense but sure. The door shut behind him, sealing in the quiet. Why wouldn't he let her help? She could manage a lot more. Ease his burden. Give her something to do to keep her thoughts far away from everyone and everything she left behind in Arizona.

GABE STOMPED OUT of Renata's yurt, the icy air pricking his skin as he pulled the door shut behind him. The warmth inside lingered against his jacket for a few seconds before surrendering to the bitter cold again. He hurried into his truck, pointing toward the barn. The website was a win. A huge step forward. But instead of easing the pressure, it tightened like a vise around his gut. One more thing checked off at the cost of another clock counting down.

Reservations could open soon. And that meant everything else needed to be ready. Lodging, food service, trails, linens, beds. The list felt endless. Renata was moving fast. Faster than him, honestly. She was stepping in, solving problems. He should be relieved. Instead, the weight of it settled deeper. Not just the guest ranch. Everything.

The morning air had a bite to it, crisp against his neck, but he hardly noticed as he crossed the short distance to the barn. The heaviness of the morning settled deeper. He felt inept. Unprepared. In over his head. By the time he saddled his horse and rode out, the motion helped. At least a little.

Haydon was already managing the cattle ranch, especially since he'd been gone in Arizona. Now, he had to say the words to make it official. Because he needed at least this one thing off his plate. He pulled his reins slightly, slowing as his horse crested the ridge overlooking the far pasture. Midmorning sunlight stretched long and golden over the hills, melting the last traces of frost clinging to the grass. Good riding weather. Or at least, good enough to make this ride useful.

Haydon rode beside him, posture easy in the saddle, scanning the herd scattered below. She didn't waste time second-guessing things. That's why this handoff needed to happen now. Even though he had planned to step back, the reality sat heavier than he wanted to admit. This land had shaped him, its rhythms lived in his bones. Letting it go should have felt like relief. Instead, it felt like losing a part of himself.

But Haydon had proven time and again that she could handle it. She saw what needed to be done without waiting for instructions, caught problems before they started, moved through the work like she'd been leading it for years. She could do this. He just had to step aside. His fingers tightened briefly around the reins before he forced them to relax. Just one thing off his plate. Just one decision that had to be made. So why did it feel like he was leaving behind more than just responsibility?

"This ranch has always been cattle first," he said, voice

quieter than he meant.

Haydon snorted. "Maybe when Papa ran it. Not anymore."

Gabe's gut pinched, and he pressed his lips together. She wasn't wrong. The quiet stretched between them, only broken by the rhythmic crunch of hooves against the frozen grass. Haydon had managed for weeks without him. She was ready, even if a part of him wasn't.

"You ready to take over the cattle ranch management? For good?"

She inched her cowgirl hat a little higher on her head. "Been doing it."

He nodded. "Good job of it, too."

A snort escaped her lips. "You don't like letting things go, do you?"

Her words landed hard, but true. "Fair enough."

"I've got this, Gabe."

He shifted slightly in the saddle, adjusting his grip on the reins, but the tension in his shoulders didn't ease. "I know."

Finally, Haydon glanced at him, voice even. "Guest ranch is coming together faster than expected. Renata's got a handle on things."

Gabe nodded automatically. Renata. She was the reason things were moving at all. She was pushing forward, staying on top of details he hadn't even thought about yet.

"She's gonna need real independence if she's running this side of things," Haydon added. "You gotta let her take the reins."

Haydon's words pressed in, solid and unshakable. He knew that. Gabe swallowed, pushing a hand through his hair, gaze shifting toward the barn. "She doesn't have a way to get to town."

Haydon frowned slightly, like she knew where this was headed but wasn't saying it yet. The thought thickened the air. Unresolved. His eyes landed on Vern's truck, untouched since winter, since everything changed. The keys were still inside the barn.

"She'd take care of it," Gabe murmured. "She'll need it."

A beat. Then Haydon nodded. Decision made.

Gabe guided his horse into a steady trot, pushing forward, even as something deep shifted inside him. The quiet acknowledgment that Renata was becoming part of this place, whether he wanted to think about it yet. As they reached the main barn, he swung down from the saddle, the harsh chill sinking deeper into his bones. He ran a hand along his horse's flank before stepping toward the workbench, eyes locking onto Vern's keys hanging from their usual hook. His fingers closed over them, cool metal against his palm. One problem solved. More waiting. More than he could count still left. At least this one he could fix.

Gabe pulled into the clearing near Renata's yurt, shutting off the truck as he caught sight of her near the porch, sweeping dust and dead leaves off it. He stepped out, boots pressing into the dirt where frost hadn't fully melted.

"Got something for you."

Renata startled slightly, turning toward him with narrowed eyes. Her hair was pulled into a loose ponytail, strands slipping free in the morning wind. She looked comfortable, in control. That unsettled him more than it should have.

"Oh?" she muttered, brushing hair out of her face.

Gabe huffed a quiet laugh, shaking his head. "You need to go into town."

Confusion flickered before settling into quiet curiosity. "For supplies?"

"For everything," he clarified. "Furniture, hardware, whatever you need to finish this yurt for the website."

She considered him, eyes scanning his face like she was trying to gauge whether he had an ulterior motive. He didn't. At least, not one that he'd admit. She tucked the broom and dustpan inside. Then she locked the door and followed him to his truck.

Instead of heading straight into town, Gabe drove to the barn. The familiar shape of Vern's truck still parked where it had sat untouched for months. Renata frowned slightly as he cut the engine. "Why are we here?"

Gabe leaned back, exhaling once before turning toward her. "You need your own transportation if you're gonna handle the guest ranch efficiently," he said simply, reaching into his jacket pocket, fingers gripping the keys. She straightened slightly. Her gaze dropped to his hand as he turned the keys over in his palm, a slow, deliberate movement before extending them toward her.

He hesitated before handing over the keys. "How long are you planning to stay?"

Renata's fingers closed around the metal. "Dalton's been understanding about my... situation. But he'll need me back soon. A few weeks, maybe."

"Weeks," Gabe repeated, something cold settling in his gut. A few weeks. Not months. Not indefinitely. Just enough time to get the guest ranch open. Then she'd be gone.

She nodded, her gaze dropping to the keys in her palm. He watched her fingers curl around them, noting the way she didn't quite meet his eyes. Like she was wrestling with something she couldn't voice.

A beat of silence stretched between them. Renata stared at the keys, and he could see the hesitation in the set of her shoulders before she spoke, quiet but certain. "This was Vern's."

Gabe nodded once. "Yeah."

He watched understanding flicker across her features, the weight of what he was offering settling into her expression. Then, without overthinking it, she pocketed the keys.

The simple gesture hit him harder than it should have. Because somehow, giving her Vern's keys felt like giving her a piece of the guest ranch operation itself. A piece of himself. Even if it was only temporary.

Gabe followed behind her as she drove over to her yurt. She parked Vern's truck, then they headed into town together. The road stretched ahead, long and winding, the silence between them not uncomfortable, but charged with unspoken anticipation. It was the first time they'd been alone, away from the ranch. No schedules, no obligations pressing in. Just distance and the quiet sense of whatever had been growing between them.

Renata rested her arm against the truck door, gaze flicking between thinning trees and open pasture. Gabe noticed how easily she fit here now, like she wasn't just passing through, but settling in.

"This is new," she murmured after a while. "You and me. Off ranch property."

Gabe smirked slightly, eyes staying on the road. "Don't get used to it."

Her laugh was soft. Unfiltered. Almost easy. His chest eased, the tension lifting. He'd missed that sound.

The landscape gradually morphed as they neared town. Open fields gave way to scattered buildings, side roads meandering toward storefronts. A cluster of cars lined the edge of the shopping center parking lot, headlights catching in the early afternoon light. Gabe pulled into an open space near the big box store, turning off the truck.

Renata reached for the door handle, her focus already on the storefronts ahead. He could see it. The way her expression sharpened, the way she was mentally sorting through what needed to be done. Planning. Preparing. Solving problems before they even fully formed. Gabe exhaled slowly, glancing toward her. It wasn't just her presence he was noticing anymore. It was everything about her, the way she steeped herself in his world with quiet certainty. She wasn't just making things easier. She was making them possible.

"This one's decent," she murmured. "Doesn't scream temporary."

Gabe studied her choices. They were not just for function, but for permanence. "You sure it'll fit in the yurt?"

She smirked. "Guess we'll find out."

Something about that answer, about her certainty, about her moving forward without hesitation, caused his chest to expand. They grabbed end tables, lamps, and an easy chair. All practical, all meant to turn the yurt into something livable, something that felt like a place someone stayed for more than a handful of nights.

After purchasing the furniture, they walked down to the big box store, wandering through the aisles. Renata spotted the curtain section and walked to the display racks. "Kinda bright," she mused, running her fingers along one panel, expression thoughtful. "But the yurt needs some color. Something soft to balance all the wood."

Gabe exhaled, hands settling into his pockets. "You've thought this through."

Her gaze met his, unwavering and calm, carrying a depth he couldn't look away from. "I have."

That was what got him. The certainty, the ease with which she was making this space her own. As they loaded the cart, she gave him a sideways glance.

"I've got an idea for the rest of the decor."

Gabe lifted a brow. "Oh?"

She shrugged. "Yard sales. People get rid of amazing pieces all the time. Art, mirrors, random things that give a place character."

A chuckle escaped him, unfiltered, unexpected. "Yard sales?"

She grinned. "You think everything has to be bought shiny and new? With some spray paint and crafty touch-ups, I can make some old pictures and decor work."

He shook his head, amusement bubbling in his chest. It wasn't the yard sales. It was her. It was the way she found solutions without hesitation, the way she saw possibilities where other people saw scraps.

"It's smart," he admitted, pushing the cart forward.

"You'll have to show me how this treasure hunting works."

Her smile lingered, easy, like she knew he'd just admitted to something bigger than thrift shopping.

Gabe eased the cart forward, eyeing the checkout ahead. Renata studied the impulse-buy shelves full of packs of batteries, brightly colored keychains, a display of half-priced winter gloves. She already cataloged which ones were actually useful. That's when he saw it. A pair of soft, lined slippers, the kind meant for both indoor and outdoor wear, tucked against a display of blankets. The memory hit fast. Her bare feet near the wood stove, the way she pulled her coat around herself like a robe. A solution.

Before he could overthink it, he muttered, "I'll be right back."

She barely glanced at him, nodding absently, still focused on the shelves. Gabe stepped away, weaving through a few aisles, passing stacks of throw blankets and overpriced candles before he spotted it. The robe. Warm. Thick. Not flashy. Just the kind of thing someone reached for without thinking, without hesitating, something meant to be worn.

He didn't question himself. Didn't second-guess the impulse. He took both to the nearest register, paid, tucked them into the bag before she could see, then headed back to where she stood. She barely registered his return, nudging the cart forward as the cashier motioned them ahead. She had no idea. And somehow, he liked that. The weight of it in the bag, the quiet act of choosing comfort for her, without being asked.

They loaded the truck. Boxes stacked, shopping bags tucked into corners, the couch wedged in at just the right angle. Gabe secured the last strap, the rough edge of nylon biting into his palm. The cold pressed into his jacket, the light stretching thinner toward dusk. He glanced at Renata, watching the way she adjusted the last buckle, careful, methodical, like she understood the importance of the moment even when she didn't say it outright.

She had a way of tucking herself into places, into moments, into lives without force, without pretense. And that should have unsettled him. It didn't. If anything, it made him wonder when he stopped seeing her as someone passing through and started seeing her as someone staying. As someone who belonged.

Gabe exhaled, flexing his fingers against the chill. "Let's get this back to the yurt," he murmured, reaching for the driver's side door.

Renata nodded, brushing a stray hair from her face, already turning toward the passenger seat, already fitting herself into this moment like she had every other one before it. Like she'd always been here.

13

A WEEK. SHE'D been at the Broken Spur for a week. Renata felt good about it. Mostly. She stood near the small table, fingers brushing over her planner, the neatly written lists of everything she needed to do, everything she needed to organize. Tasks. Plans. Movement. Things she could control.

She stretched, muscles sore from dusting, vacuuming, and mopping all twenty rooms of the lodge over the last two days. Gabe had been busy with a few meetings and errands in town. They went well. A smile graced her lips. She could hardly wait for the text from him the next time he entered the lodge to find how much she had accomplished. He'd be surprised. Though she figured it might be a few days before he had time to get over there. It would be worth the wait.

Her throat tickled, so she dug into her backpack purse for a lozenge. That's when her fingers brushed the fabric — soft, worn, painfully familiar. The yellow onesie. Cartoon bunnies. Tiny sleeves. Meant for a newborn. Her breath caught. Everything inside her halting at once.

Grief didn't knock. It didn't wait for permission. It knocked down doors, crashing into the quiet with sharp, unrelenting force. Her fingers curled around the onesie, breath uneven, the room suddenly too warm, too much. She inhaled sharply, pressing the fabric against her lap, fingers tracing the edge. Her chest tightened. Cliff.

She swallowed hard, closing her eyes briefly, pushing past the ache. Where was he right now? What was he doing? How much had he grown? She hoped he was happy. That Devon and Raina were happy. That he was loved. Of course, he was loved.

Renata let out a slow breath, her fingers twitching slightly, hovering over her phone. She could check the family group text. There were probably pictures. Snapshots of a life still moving forward without her. Her thumb brushed the edge of the screen. Almost. But no. Not today.

She exhaled sharply, tucking the onesie back into her bag, shoving the phone deep into her pocket, standing too fast. She couldn't sit here, not drowning, not letting herself spiral. She needed to stay busy. Do something familiar. Something that wouldn't require her to sit still and feel.

The cold hit her as soon as she stepped outside, sharp against her flushed skin, stealing the breath from her lips. She pulled her coat closer. Didn't hesitate. Her boots thumped against the dirt, each step solid beneath her, carrying her toward the truck before she could second-guess it. She barely registered the drive, just the hum of the engine.

By the time she stepped inside the ranch house, the scent of coffee lingered faintly in the air, wrapping around her like something familiar. She focused on that. On the warmth, the movement, the next step ahead. She grabbed an apron, rolling up her sleeves. She'd bake. Because she needed to. Because it was something she knew how to do. Because baking had steps. And steps meant movement. And movement meant she didn't have to sit in her thoughts.

She couldn't rewrite the past. She couldn't change what had been lost. But she could do this. At least for now.

The kitchen held the same warmth it always did. Wooden cabinets polished smooth from years of use, worn countertops. Except she had no idea where anything was. Renata sighed, tugging open drawers, scanning the contents, movements just slightly too abrupt, not impatient, but restless. Silverware. Spare batteries. Measuring spoons tucked too far back. She crossed the room to the pantry, fingers skimming the rows of labeled jars, picking up containers just to set them down again. Flour. Sugar. Cinnamon, no nutmeg.

She exhaled sharply, rolling her shoulders. At least she had something to do. She blew a breath through her nose. This shouldn't feel this hard. Finally, she found a mixing bowl in the lower cabinet, knocking over an empty pie pan in the process. The clatter echoed in the quiet, sharp, jarring. She exhaled through her nose, setting it onto the counter with more force than necessary.

Muscle memory took over. Cream butter. Stir sugar. Whisk in vanilla. The scent deepened, wafting into the air, a first trace of sweet comfort in dessert form. Routine. Predictable. She focused on the rhythm, on the process, on the familiarity, until the door swung open, laughter breaking into the space, pulling her back to the present.

Harlan and Haydon stepped in, shedding jackets, kicking off boots, their simple rhythm filling the room before she had time to steady herself. Harlan made a beeline toward the kitchen island, eyes locking on the cooling racks lined with fresh cookies. Haydon paused instead, gaze flicking toward Renata, studying her a little too carefully.

"You feeling domestic today?" she asked casually, but not without weight.

"Just needed something to do."

Renata shrugged, lifting a cookie from the tray and handing it to Harlan. He stuffed a few in his pockets before pushing away from the counter, already heading toward the barn, mumbling something about finishing chores before dinner. She barely registered it.

Haydon hummed softly. Didn't push. Didn't pry. But didn't let it go entirely, either. Renata wiped her hands on a dish towel, avoiding Haydon's gaze, fingers unsteady. Haydon didn't speak at first, just watched, just waited, the quiet stretching long enough that Renata felt exposed without a word being said.

Then, gently, "You okay?"

Renata swallowed hard, reaching for her purse, fingers trembling slightly as she pulled out the onesie. She didn't look at Haydon. Couldn't.

"I don't, I don't understand," she whispered, voice barely holding. She shook the onesie lightly, as if the fabric itself might offer answers. "How could He..." Her breath caught. "How could God just let me..." Her throat burned. Her pulse roared in her ears. "...love a baby that wasn't my own?"

The onesie crumpled in her grip, and for a second, her entire body felt too small to contain everything pressing against her ribs.

Haydon was quiet for a long moment. Not dismissing. Not rushing. Then, gently, she pulled out a chair, not forcing but inviting Renata to settle. Renata didn't want to sit. Didn't want to talk. But her legs didn't feel steady anymore. So she sat.

She gripped the onesie tighter, knuckles whitening, pulse thrumming. "I thought I was doing God's will," she murmured, voice barely above breath. "Being a surrogate for them. I must have gotten it wrong."

Haydon's eyes didn't waver. "Why?" she asked, low, steady. "What makes you think you got it wrong?"

Haydon's words hung in the air, solid, immovable, nothing quick, nothing easy. Renata wanted to push them away. Wanted to argue. Wanted to say no, this suffering isn't some lesson I needed to learn. Instead, her breath shook.

She squeezed the onesie, fingers pressing deep into the worn fabric. The ache inside her didn't shrink. It stretched heavier, fuller, demanding space. The truth was, she didn't want to understand this yet.

Renata exhaled sharply, clenching the onesie against her chest. "This. This pain." Her voice cracked. "This utter..." The words wouldn't form. Her throat tightened too much, her ribs too hollow. Her breath trembled. "Devastation I feel." She exhaled shakily, gripping the edge of the table, fingers pressing into the wood as if she could pull herself back together by touch alone. "How could this be God's plan for me?"

Haydon's voice remained steady. "We weren't promised easy."

Renata let out a slow breath, staring down at the fabric, her thumb absently tracing the outline of the cartoon bunny along the sleeve. She shook her head, barely. "That doesn't make it fair."

Haydon's expression remained placid, not dismissing, not offering false comfort. "Fair wasn't promised either."

The words lodged deep, sitting heavily in the space between them. Renata's pulse pressed hard on her wrists. She didn't speak. Didn't know how. She closed her eyes briefly, inhaling sharply. The lingering sweet scent of cookies was at odds with her churning soul.

Haydon's voice softened, but the weight never left it. "Maybe grief itself wasn't the plan. Maybe it was." Renata's breath hitched. She didn't move. Didn't blink. The ache inside her twisted deep, relentless. Then, slowly, her palm pressed against the onesie, smoothing out the wrinkles, as if she could press herself back into something whole again.

Haydon continued, gently but firmly. "Maybe He's using it to grow something stronger in you. Or maybe it's so you could understand Christ's love, the depth and breadth of it in a new way, as a mother. As a woman who made the unthinkable sacrifice."

Renata sat still. She wasn't ready to say Haydon was right. But she wasn't ready to say she was wrong, either. The ache inside her felt just as sharp. But now it was tangled with unsettled heaviness. No peace. Not yet. But maybe a beginning.

THE DOOR TO the yurt was ajar, warmth spilling into the crisp afternoon, carrying hints of cedar and fresh linen. Gabe stepped inside, blinking against the soft light filtering through the bare windows, except they wouldn't be bare for long. Renata stood balanced on a stepladder, stretching upward, drill in hand, jaw set in concentration.

He stopped just inside the threshold. She hadn't noticed him yet. That shouldn't have mattered. But it did. She leaned forward, adjusting the bracket near the top of the frame. The ladder wobbled, just enough to make him rush over. His hands steadied it before she lost balance. Her breath hitched.

Renata blinked down at him, breath uneven. "You always sneak up on people like this?"

Gabe huffed a quiet laugh, adjusting his grip on the ladder. "Only when they look like they're about to fall."

Her lips parted slightly, like she wanted to challenge that, but she didn't. Just nodded once, gaze lingering a fraction too long. Her fingers hesitated on the drill. Something was bothering her. The sorrow etched deep in her eyes. He figured it was the reason three dozen cookies appeared in his kitchen a few hours ago.

"Haydon mentioned you talked." His voice was quiet but steady. No pressure. Just offering her space to say what she wanted.

Renata let out a slow breath, balancing the drill on the top step of the ladder. She picked up one of the screws for the curtain bracket, rubbing it between her thumb and index finger. The silence stretched. Then, her voice came softly, uncertain. "I've been wondering if... if God had a purpose for all of it."

She didn't say pain outright. Didn't say loss. But Gabe heard it anyway. Felt it in the way she fidgeted with the screw, making no move to finish installing the curtain rod.

"And?" he asked.

Renata stared out the window, expression unreadable. "I don't know yet. Maybe He does." Then she let out a breath. Not relief, not resolution, just acceptance. Glancing toward him, she offered a small, quiet smile. Not peace. Not yet. But maybe something close.

"Guess I better finish this," she said, picking up the drill again.

Gabe took her hands, his thumb brushing her knuckles. "The grief. I know. Losing my parents... It was hard. Still miss them. But, yeah, in time, it will hurt less."

"I just..." She shrugged. "Didn't expect... I don't know."

Gabe wanted to pull her into his arms. To offer comfort. To ease her pain. Instead, he coaxed her off the stepladder and picked up the drill before he finished the pilot holes for the brackets.

They moved in sync after that, aware of each small touch. Renata passed him screws, their fingers brushing. Gabe adjusted the rod while she held the other end, her presence filling his space. He could have ignored the awareness, should have, but it had already settled deep.

When they finally finished hanging the rod, the curtain fabric settled against the window, catching the light, casting the room in a softer glow. Renata exhaled, stepping back, hands on her hips. Gabe watched her, his heart picking up pace as a satisfied smile stretched across her lips.

"I love it!"

Her smile lit her face, and something inside him sparked, too. He held her gaze as currents pinged between them. She was so beautiful.

After a beat, Gabe motioned toward the unopened end table boxes, brow lifting slightly. Renata smirked. "I was debating it. But since you're here..."

He exhaled through his nose, shaking his head, rolling up his sleeves before grabbing the first box. They worked in sync, no rush, no need for conversation. Renata read the instructions cross-legged on the floor, passing him screws and brackets. Each brush of fingers felt natural now, familiar. Like she belonged in his space.

They assembled the tables, dropped the new rug into place, adjusted lamps and shelving—small things, but things that made it homey. After tightening the last bolt, Renata sat back, stretching her legs out. "That's progress."

Gabe scanned the room, taking in the subtle warmth that hadn't been here before, the way each touch made the space feel lived-in, intentional. "You weren't joking about making this place photo-ready," he murmured.

Renata's lips tugged into something pleased. "Speaking of, River sent me the finished website link yesterday. I've been adding property pictures."

Gabe straightened, brows lifting. "Already?"

She pulled out her laptop, tapping a few keys before turning the screen toward him. And Gabe stared. The homepage loaded, the ranch name, Broken Spur Guest Ranch, stretching across a sweeping shot of the open land at golden hour, light settling over the hills, deepening the richness of the landscape. A custom logo adorned the upper left corner, with old style spurs.

Then more images. The barn. The lodge. When did she find time to place barrel shaped planters on the porch? The creek cutting through the back acreage. And then the exterior of the yurt. Warm light glowed from inside, inviting, steady, like it belonged here as much as anything else.

The site wasn't just polished. It was stunning. The kind of place people would look at and want to be part of. And he had Renata to thank for it. She had turned into the answer to prayers he hadn't known to ask. In more ways than one.

"This looks..." He exhaled, studying the way she tucked her legs beneath her, waiting for his reaction. "Good?" she teased.

Gabe let out a quiet breath. "Better than good."

Something proud flickered across her face. Soft. Quiet.

Like this had been hers to build, hers to piece together, and now she was seeing him recognize it in full.

Renata tapped at the trackpad, scrolling through the finished site. "Looks professional," Gabe admitted, still a little stunned at how polished it all was.

"Thank you," she said, smirking slightly. "But it's missing something."

He lifted a brow. "What's that?"

She angled the laptop toward him, motioning to the About section. "A picture of the owner."

He exhaled a short laugh. "Not necessary."

Renata hummed like she wasn't convinced. Then, before he could protest, she grabbed her phone. And snapped a picture. Gabe blinked. "Renata." Another picture. She grinned outright, her finger already swiping across the screen, syncing them to the cloud before he could react.

He narrowed his eyes. "At least let me see them."

She held her phone just out of reach, lips twitching in amusement. "Mm... nope."

He huffed, reaching for it, but she angled away, laughing softly. "They better not be awful," he muttered.

"They're great," she assured him, still looking far too pleased with herself.

Gabe shook his head, sighing because he knew, deep down, she wasn't going to let him see them anytime soon. Something about the moment lingered, like she'd captured more than he was ready to see.

"Thanks for the assist."

He nodded, turning toward the door, hand brushing the frame as he stepped out. "I have a feeling you didn't actually need it."

She smiled, small but knowing. "Maybe. But I didn't mind it either."

As he stepped outside, pulling the door closed behind him, the cold air did little to steady the warmth still pressing against his chest. She wasn't just helping. She wasn't just fixing things. She was becoming his entire world. And he wasn't prepared for it. Not at all.

Gabe opened the truck door but paused, the moment pressing deep, unexpected yet undeniable. His gaze landed on the bag behind the seat. Forgotten last week, but now? Now felt right. So he grabbed the shopping bag and jogged back up the porch stairs. The familiar heft of it in his grip reminded him how warm it had looked when he bought it.

He knocked once before opening the door. Renata looked up, eyes flickering with a mix of surprise and — dare he hope — joy.

"I thought you left."

He grinned, but it felt different this time. Felt like warm sunshine exploding in his chest just at the sight of her. He'd only been gone for a minute, tops. He held out the bag. "Got you something."

Renata blinked, her gaze flicking from his to the bag. Curiosity pulled her closer. She eased it open, fingers brushing first against the soft-lined slippers. Then the robe. She didn't speak. Didn't move. Just stared down at them, fingers lingering against the fabric, breath catching just slightly.

Gabe shifted his weight, suddenly too aware of the moment stretching between them. Too aware of how much he wanted her to feel what this meant. Wanted her to know. Wanted — *Lord help me* — to kiss her, to pour everything into it, to show her what sat in his chest like an ache, like an answer. But now wasn't the time. Not for her.

So instead, he swallowed, his voice lower now, rough around the edges. "You were barefoot," he said. "And using your coat as a robe. Figured this might work better."

Renata exhaled sharply, something flickering across her face, not just gratitude, but something deeper, something unguarded. Then, without thinking, without hesitation, she stepped forward, wrapping her arms around him, pressing in close.

It was fast, instinctive, a silent thank-you, but also more

than that. Gabe barely had time to react, his breath hitching, his hands hovering at her waist before settling, before holding her there. Not rushing. Not pulling away. She smelled like cinnamon and soap, warmth and sunshine, and her exhale softened against his chest. Just for a second, just enough.

It should have been fleeting. But somehow, she didn't pull back immediately. And somehow, he didn't let go, either. Then, slowly, too slowly, Renata leaned back. Her fingers lifted gently, skimming up, settling against his cheek. And held, steady, warm, a quiet claim. And held. Tethering him there, eyes locked on hers, on this undeniable connection taking deep root between them.

He lost count of the beats. Only knew that she was looking at him like she saw everything, like she saw him, like she understood more than he was ready to say aloud. Like she wasn't afraid of it. But he was. Because he wanted more. Wanted to kiss her. Wanted her to know how deep this ran in him. But now wasn't the time. Not for her.

So he swallowed again, throat tight, breath uneven as he gently, so gently, wrapped his fingers around hers, lifting her hand from his cheek. Held it for a beat. Just one. Then let go.

He cleared his throat, hands falling away, angling toward the door. "I'll see you tomorrow," he said, voice not quite as even as he wanted it to be.

Renata pressed her fingers into the fabric of the robe, thumb skimming the edge, like she wasn't quite ready to let go of the moment. Then, finally, she nodded. "Yeah," she murmured. "Tomorrow."

Gabe let out a slow breath, adjusting his stance. Leaving wasn't simple, not now. Fingers closed around the handle, but he didn't turn it yet. Renata stood there, soft, unreadable, holding him in place just for a second. Then, too soon, he stepped into the cold. It hit fast, biting deep. But that wasn't what he noticed most.

14

A FEW DAYS later, Renata woke, stuffing her feet into the soft, cozy slippers. Then she donned the plush robe, immediately warmed against the coolness that settled into the yurt each morning. She rubbed the lapel of the robe against her cheek, savoring the gifts from Gabe. She doubted he knew just how much they meant to her. The robe and slippers hinted at more than just a temporary season to help him set up the Broken Spur Guest Ranch.

They were useless gifts for someone returning to Arizona who barely needed a light sweater in the sunny winter. They were perfect gifts for someone staying in Montana who needed to ward off the chill of winter.

Renata padded down to the wood stove, adding another split log, like Gabe had showed her. Then she set about her morning routine. As she hung the robe on its hook, her fingers lingered on the fabric. Its softness reminded her of the tender look in Gabe's silver-blue eyes when he gave it to her. Her stomach swooped at the memory. She thought he wanted to kiss her.

At first, it frightened her. He was a cowboy. Just like Jace Tanner. Except he was nothing like her two-timing ex. Gabe Braxton was an amazing man. Gentle and kind when the moment called for it. Sensitive to what she needed, even when she had no words to articulate her needs. Like in the two-day drive up from Arizona.

Then there was his thoughtful consideration. The way he weighed options carefully, decided, and moved forward. His wisdom reminded her of her father. Renata tucked her feet into her cowgirl boots and donned her cowgirl hat, wondering what her parents would think of Gabe. She didn't recall them meeting him when he was in Arizona. Or maybe they had met him briefly at the hospital when they came to visit her. Much of that time was a blur, one that still hurt too much to linger on.

The rumble of Gabe's truck sounded outside, so she squared her shoulders, picked up her backpack purse and opened the door. His instant smile warmed away any cold swirling around her as she slid into the passenger seat of his truck.

"You ready to find some treasures for the lodge?"

The skin around his eyes crinkled slightly as his cheeks, clean-shaven again, pushed higher with his smile. His after-shave filled the cab, sending her pulse racing.

"Teach me, oh Jedi Master."

Renata snorted. "I didn't picture you as a Star Wars fan."

He reached over and squeezed her hand. "There are a few things you have yet to learn about me."

Either it was the heat of his hand, or the prospect of spending enough time with him to learn everything about him, that sent tingles rolling through her body. When he placed his hand on the shifter to back out, she missed his touch. Yeah, he was nothing—not a thing—like Jace.

"Where to first?"

Renata pulled up the yard sale announcements and set the navigation on her phone to guide them to the first address. "This is a community sale, so we should find several in this area."

Once Gabe turned on to the main road, he wrapped his hand around hers. She curled her fingers around his, savoring the connection. "I saw what you did in the lodge."

Her cheeks warmed. "When did you clean everything?"

She puffed her cheeks before she blew out a soft breath. "Five days ago?"

Gabe cringed. "Guess I should have noticed before yesterday morning."

She giggled. "Maybe."

"How long did it take?"

"About two days."

He squeezed her hand. "Thanks for doing that. And for... Everything."

"Of course. Happy to help."

And Renata was. Happy to help him. Glad for the change of scenery. Grateful for the time to heal. Excited to explore his beautiful ranch. Thrilled to uncover hidden gems with him at many yard sales.

Gabe pulled into the first stop. S neat row of folding tables lined with mismatched chairs, stacks of books, and an assortment of knickknacks. Renata scanned the setup, already spotting potential gems among the clutter. Gabe, on the other hand, frowned, his gaze bouncing between a chipped vase and a rusted metal sign for motor oil.

"You're sure this is worth it?" he muttered, eyeing the tables like they might personally offend him.

Renata bit back a laugh. "Absolutely. Yard sales are all about finding hidden treasures."

"Right." He nodded once, serious. "Like—" He pointed to an old coffee tin labeled Grandma's Secret Cookie Recipe.

She smirked. "Not quite."

His eyes narrowed at her amusement. "Okay, then, teach me, oh Master of Discounted Odds and Ends."

Renata stifled a giggle, steering him toward an antique mirror tucked behind a stack of old vinyl records. "This is what you want to look for," she said, lifting the mirror and showing him the intricate wooden frame, worn but still elegant.

He rubbed his jaw, studying it. "So it's all about finding

things that look... fancy?"

"Not always," she said, setting it aside carefully. "It's about finding pieces that add character. Things with history. And potential."

He looked around, then reached for an old cowboy figurine missing half an arm. "Character?"

Renata laughed. "Depends. If you want a one-armed ranch mascot, sure."

Gabe huffed a quiet chuckle, setting the figurine back down. "I see you're enjoying this."

She grinned. "You bet I am."

Still smiling, she turned toward another table, only to realize Gabe wasn't following. He was watching her. Just watching. The playful warmth between them shifted, stretched, held. And for a second, the yard sale disappeared. Just him, just her, just the way he was looking at her like she was the most interesting find here. Her breath caught.

This felt too domestic, too couple-like. Renata forced herself to remember this was temporary. She was helping a friend, not playing house with the man whose smile made her forget every reason she should go back to Arizona.

Gabe cleared his throat, gaze flicking back toward the tables. "Fine. Show me your ways. Let's find some treasures."

The moment broke, but something lingered in the air. Renata exhaled, shaking off the spell and stepping forward.

"First lesson," she said, nudging his arm. "Don't call them treasures unless you actually commit to finding the good stuff."

Gabe grinned, reaching for another item at random. Renata groaned.

"Okay, cowboy," she teased. "That's a toaster from 1996. We're going to need to work on your instincts."

GABE HAD NO idea why he was here. Well, no, that wasn't true. He was here because Renata was here, because she had some grand idea about finding "hidden treasures" to make the lodge and yurts feel more lived-in, more inviting. But looking around, he was pretty sure all he saw were piles of things people wanted to get rid of.

Yet Renata? She lit up, eyes scanning the rows of mismatched furniture and tattered books, like she was searching for gold in a pan of dirt. Gabe crossed his arms, leaning against the truck, watching her talk animatedly with the seller, asking about the history of a carved wooden box. She was in her element here. Fully alive, fully engaged, fully the kind of person who saw beauty where others saw junk.

And maybe that was why he stayed quiet. Because he liked watching her like this. Even if he wasn't sold on the whole yard sale thing.

She held up an antique mirror. "This is perfect!"

He glanced at the $45 price tag, his jaw tightening slightly. Every dollar mattered with the loan payments looming. But seeing her face light up... "Yeah. Let's get it."

Renata turned, grinning at him, lifting the box slightly. "This is handmade, Gabe."

"Look at the detail."

She leaned closer to show him the carved box, her shoulder brushing his arm. The faint scent of her shampoo filled his senses, distracting him from the woodwork. He cleared his throat. "Right. Detail."

Gabe pretended to examine it, but really, he was examining her. The way she bounced on her heels, energy infectious, a smile pulling him closer before he even realized he was moving. He rubbed his jaw. "You're really enjoying this, huh?"

She rolled her eyes. "Because I have taste."

"You sure about that?" He picked up a horrendously faded rooster figurine from the next table.

Renata gasped, mock horror in her voice. "That is offensive to my yard sale integrity."

He smirked, setting it down, watching her move to another table, scanning items with a trained eye he didn't quite understand yet. It wasn't just buying things. It was curating something meaningful, giving old things a new purpose. Like making the Broken Spur into something new. Him too. And that did something to him.

Gabe exhaled, rolling his shoulders, and decided maybe, just maybe, he'd give this a fair shot.

A few finds later, an antique mirror, a framed black-and-white big sky ranch photo, and a sturdy old lantern. He had to admit, she was onto something. And then he saw it. Not on a table. Not up for sale. Just Renata. Laughing, flipping her cowgirl hat back slightly, teasing him over the fact that he kept picking "the ugliest possible things on purpose."

He hadn't been trying to point them out. Just trying to learn. But after that little dig, he started doing it on purpose.

When they stopped at the next house, his truck filling quickly, Gabe watched as Renata practically sprinted toward a stack of framed pictures, her boots kicking up dust on the gravel driveway.

"Oh my gosh, Gabe, these are perfect!"

She lifted one of the frames, revealing a striking image of a grizzly mid-stride, muscles tensed, fur rippling in golden light. "Look at them!" she gushed, flipping through a whole collection of six different grizzly bear photos. One standing in a river, another roaring, a cub peering curiously from behind a tree.

Gabe rubbed his jaw, lips twitching. "That's... a lot of bears."

Renata huffed dramatically, leaning the frames against her leg. "They are majestic, Gabe."

"Uh-huh." He picked up a seventh frame she hadn't grabbed yet, this one of a grizzly scratching its back against a tree.

Renata snorted. "Okay, maybe not majestic in that one. But still! I'll spray paint the frames, clean the glass. We can make an entire section of the lodge the Grizzly Rooms!"

Gabe chuckled, shaking his head, amused by how quickly she'd committed to the idea. "Grizzly Rooms," he echoed. "Are we warning guests, or just hoping they find it charming?"

Renata flicked her gaze toward him, the slow raise of her brow, and deliberately paused before she spoke. "They will love it."

He fought back a grin. "You sure? Because I've heard people check out of hotels over bad wallpaper, so an entire wing dedicated to bears might be a risk."

Renata pointed a finger at him in mock accusation. "You, sir, are underestimating the grandeur of Montana wildlife."

"I'm just saying, not everyone wants to sleep with grizzlies watching them."

"It's not like they are taxidermic trophies," she said, flipping her hair, already loading the pictures into the truck before he could protest further. "They're just pictures."

By the time they hit the next sale, Gabe thought maybe, just maybe, she'd rein in her enthusiasm. He was wrong. The moment she spotted a hand-carved grizzly figurine, she gasped so dramatically the seller jumped.

"Oh, this is coming home with us," she declared.

Gabe lifted a brow. "'Us'?"

"For the lodge," she said, rolling her eyes like he should already be on board. She looked so pretty when her cheeks flushed.

And then came the fishing-themed pieces at yet another yard sale. A rustic framed print of a trout leaping from a river, an old tackle box, a set of vintage fishing lures mounted behind glass. Renata inspected them like a museum curator. "These can go in the Fishing Rooms!"

Gabe groaned. "There are themed rooms now?"

"Oh, don't act like you don't love it," she teased, nudging him with her elbow.

Gabe huffed a quiet laugh, shaking his head as she paid for the fishing decor without hesitation. Then, just as they finished packing up the last find, her phone rang. She turned away, answering quickly, her voice changing from light to tense.

Gabe leaned against the truck, watching her, watching the shift in her shoulders, the small sigh she barely let out. And that was when he realized it. The truest treasure today wasn't the pictures, or the carved bears or the fishing lures. It was her. Glowing. Unstoppable. A force he couldn't look away from. Vibrant, completely in her element, completely breathtaking. And she didn't even know it.

And as she walked further away to take her call, something settled deep inside him. The quiet, unwavering truth that he hadn't just fallen for her. He had lost his heart completely.

15

RENATA GLANCED AT her phone, and her stomach clenched, stealing every last ounce of the joy she'd built in the last few hours with Gabe. Dalton. Her cousin. Her boss. She hadn't called him since she left Arizona.

"I need to take this," she said before stepping away from Gabe.

"Hello?"

"Rennie. How are you doing?"

She heard the strain in his voice. "Fine."

"How's your vacation?"

Renata stifled a snort before it escaped. "Fine. How can I help?"

Dalton cleared his throat. "It's almost the end of May."

She walked down the sidewalk several paces and turned to watch Gabe barter with the seller. She had known this day would come. And soon. Didn't mean she was ready for it. Ready to have this conversation with Dalton.

"I'm aware."

"Rennie, when are you coming back?"

She opened her mouth. But no words came. She should have had an answer. She should have known. Instead, silence stretched, until she finally exhaled and admitted the truth.

"I don't know." She really didn't. Montana was growing on her. A certain cowboy with silver-blue eyes was too.

The soft thud of Dalton's truck door closing sounded over the earpiece before the background noise silenced. "Listen. I know you've been through a lot."

She let out a short, humorless breath. He had no idea.

"But it's been five weeks. With Solana's morning sickness—"

"What?" Renata gasped. Her heart stuttered. A baby? Her sister hadn't said a word. No text. No call. The hurt coiled deep, tightening something in her chest.

"She didn't tell you?"

"No."

Dalton exhaled loudly. "Look, Mami and Jody are filling in for her when she doesn't feel well, but Jody's a mom, too. Shuttling kids to and from school. Just like Solana."

Jody? The spa manager was helping? "Where's Terri?"

"She's working the front desk six days a week right now."

Renata's hand flew to her forehead, knocking her cowgirl hat off kilter as she pressed her fingers to her skin. "I interviewed someone for weekends and a few evenings. But, Rennie, I need to know when you're coming home."

Home. The word slammed against her chest hard, like a sledgehammer. She involuntarily took a step back. When had Arizona stopped feeling like home?

"I'm... Not sure."

Dalton's muffled groan rang in her ears. "Don't make me do this, Rennie."

"Do what?"

"I need you back in a week, Renata. No excuses."

She heard the unspoken "or else" as if he had said it. Would he really fire her?

"Look, Dalton, I've worked for the family since I graduated high school. I hardly take vacation most years—"

"We've got a big group of athletes coming for most of June."

Her eyes rounded. "How big?"

"Fill up every available room big. That's why I can't wait any longer, Rennie. I need you back next week. No more extensions."

The old Renata would have been thrilled. They usually shut down from June to September due to the heat. Winning such a huge block of business in an off-season month… That was fantastic news. So why did she feel as if her world was crumbling around her?

"I can't leave. Gabe is opening his guest ranch the first week of June."

"You work for me. Not Gabe Braxton."

Renata's pulse hammered against her chest, and her face heated. Dalton was really going to fire her? For years, she'd given everything to the resort. Her time, her energy, her heart. And yet, after all the loyalty, after all the sacrifices, she was disposable. She was just an employee. Nothing more.

"Sort it out, Rennie. I need an answer tomorrow."

The line went dead. She tucked her phone in her coat pocket and bent low. Placing her hands on her thighs, she gasped for breath. This couldn't be happening. She didn't want to have to choose between her family's business and Gabe's. Gabe needed her. And that's when she realized it. She needed Montana. She needed Gabe. But it was more than that. She needed a life that wasn't built on sacrificing herself to hold up everyone else.

GABE'S HANDS GRIPPED the steering wheel tighter than they needed to. Not because of the drive. He could navigate these winding roads half-asleep and blindfolded if it came to it. No, the tension had nothing to do with the road. It had everything to do with Renata.

One second, she'd been laughing, flipping her cowgirl hat back, teasing him over his terrible yard sale instincts. The next, after that phone call, she'd gone quiet. Stiff. Detached. Gabe flicked a glance her way. She was staring out the window, fingers tapping absently against her knee, eyes unfocused. Something was wrong. And Gabe hated he didn't know what it was.

Renata had been laughing, teasing him, lighting up every space they walked into. But now? She was quiet, withdrawn. Like something had pulled her back into herself, away from the warmth they'd built today.

He let the silence stretch for a few more miles, waiting. Watching. Finally, keeping his tone easy, he said, "You went quiet after that call."

Renata blinked, like she'd forgotten he was sitting right next to her. She stilled for a moment, exhaling too carefully, like she was weighing how much she could say without revealing too much. "Just family stuff."

Gabe nodded slowly, keeping his voice steady, patient. "Bad news?"

She hesitated. Too long. "No, nothing like that."

But she still wasn't looking at him. And Gabe knew enough to recognize when someone was holding something close, clutching it tight enough that it hurt, but not ready to release it yet.

He huffed a quiet breath. "That was not a 'just family stuff' reaction."

Renata finally turned toward him, a flicker of something unreadable in her gaze before she looked back out the window. A beat of silence. Then soft, deliberate, "It's not important right now."

Gabe didn't like that answer. But he would not push. Not yet. Instead, he let the drive settle in quietly, his eyes flicking to the pile of treasures in the back—everything secure, nothing shifting—though the only thing truly unsettled was her.

Pulling into the lodge's gravel drive, Gabe felt the weight of the silence still hanging between them. Renata had relaxed a little since the yard sale haul, but he could still feel whatever had happened in that phone call pressing at the edge of her thoughts. And for the first time in days, he wasn't sure how to reach her.

He climbed out of the truck, expecting her to head straight for the back to unload, except she stepped toward the lodge's front entrance, pushing the glass doors open and letting out a soft breath. She wasn't rushing. And for once, he let himself slow down, too.

Inside, the lodge felt different. Warmer. More complete. He glanced around, eyes narrowing slightly. Something was new. A lot of some things. All since yesterday morning. His boots scuffed softly against the hardwood as he walked through the lobby, taking in subtle changes he hadn't noticed before. The polished wood counters now held a vase full of silk flowers. A woven basket sat tucked beside the guest check-in area filled with full color brochures of his guest ranch. A framed landscape hung near the welcome sign.

All touches that weren't his. All touches that were Renata's. He didn't know how long he stood there, just taking it in. Then he turned toward the fireplace, stopping short. Something softened in his chest.

She had added flameless candles to the thick log mantle, their deep amber hues casting soft light against the gray stone. And the photos were framed images she had taken herself. Pastures at sunrise. Cattle grazing slowly across the land. The barn standing sturdy against a stretch of open sky. She had seen the ranch exactly the way he wanted people to see it. And for the first time, he realized it wasn't just him making this place what it needed to be. It was her, too.

Gabe exhaled, rubbing the back of his neck. "Didn't realize you'd done all this."

Renata glanced at him, tilting her head slightly. "Is it okay?"

He huffed quietly, shaking his head. "It's more than

okay."

Her lips parted slightly, like she hadn't expected the compliment. Like maybe she'd been bracing for something else. He swallowed, stepping closer. "You make it feel like a place people want to be."

Renata looked away for half a second, just long enough for him to notice the way her chest rose slightly, like she was steadying herself. Then she turned back, lips pressing into something resembling a smile. "I figured the lodge should reflect the ranch. It's something we did back..." Running her fingers lightly along the smooth edge of the mantle, she huffed and glanced out the window before squaring her shoulders. She angled back toward him, a strained smile on her lips.

Gabe nodded slowly, gaze lingering on her before shifting back to the photos. "You see it the way I do."

That mattered. More than he had words for. Gabe noticed the way Renata cleared her throat, like she was trying to shake off whatever weight that phone call had left on her shoulders. She nudged his shoulder, lighter now, deliberately playful, before motioning toward the hallway leading into the northern rooms.

"Alright, cowboy. The big debate. Fishing Wing or Grizzly Wing?"

Gabe chuckled, rubbing his jaw. "We have an actual debate now?"

She lifted a brow. "You've seen what we bought."

"Fair point."

He glanced toward the northern-facing windows. The view outside was mostly thick trees and glimpses of the hills beyond. "The Fishing Wing should probably go along the south side," he mused, tilting his head, thinking it through.

She nodded. "Matches the view of the pond."

They both turned toward the northern hall, assessing the space, before Renata shot him a knowing look. "You realize what this means, right?"

Gabe sighed dramatically. "I don't know what you mean."

Her grin widened. "It means the Grizzly Rooms belong here."

Gabe groaned, shaking his head. "I knew you were going to say that."

She laughed, nudging him toward the door. "Come on. Let's make it happen."

They stepped outside, cool air slipping past them, crisp with pine and earth. Gabe trailed slightly behind, watching as Renata rolled her shoulders, stretching like she was shaking off something heavy. She exhaled, adjusting her hat slightly, then, like flipping a switch, her energy returned. "This is going to look incredible," she said, motioning toward the lodge's entrance.

Good. She was easing back into the moment. Gabe grabbed one of the first frames, one of the grizzlies, and held it in front of his face as he stepped toward her. The weight of his boots thudded against the wooden floor. Deepening his voice, he growled, "Rahr!"

Renata jumped, eyes wide, then laughed, bright and real. Finally. Finally, a real laugh. Gabe lowered the frame slowly, catching her gaze, holding it for just a second too long. "You gonna make me do all the work, or are we decorating this place together?"

She shook her head, still smiling. "You are impossible."

"But entertaining."

"That's debatable."

Gabe chuckled, shaking his head as they started hauling everything into the lodge. And just like that, the tension between them unraveled.

They worked in sync, moving through one of the newly furnished guest rooms in the Grizzly Wing, arranging the pieces they'd collected from the yard sales. Renata stood at the center of the room, head tilted, arms crossed, assessing the framed grizzly photo he had just hung above the headboard. Gabe, standing behind her, was far too aware of how close they were. Close enough to feel her presence, close enough to catch the faintest scent of pine and vanilla lingering on her skin.

"Too symmetrical?" she asked, barely above a whisper.

Gabe swallowed, forcing himself to focus on the picture and not the way her voice wound through the quiet space between them. He nodded. "Yeah. Swap them so the roaring bear is on the left. Let it balance out the movement in the river shot."

Renata did as he suggested, adjusting the frame with careful precision, her fingertips brushing the edge as she stepped back. She smiled. "I think you're getting the hang of this."

Gabe shrugged, eyes holding hers, steady, sure. "I had a good teacher."

Her gaze lingered, just a beat too long, enough for something unspoken to settle between them. Everything in him ached to close the space. To pull her in, hold her, press his lips to that spot just above her collarbone where her skin looked impossibly soft.

Then a small, quiet breath. A shift. She cleared her throat, turning away, fingers brushing over the wooden-carved grizzly before setting it neatly on the nightstand. Gabe exhaled slowly, tamping down the feelings threatening to rise. Humor. Maybe that would help.

"You actually bought that thing?" he teased, nodding toward it.

She gasped, placing a hand over her heart. "Excuse me. This is a work of art."

He chuckled, shaking his head, watching as she added two smaller figurines to the desk, completing the room's rustic, wild theme. Then, grabbing the largest carved grizzly, too big for the room, they carried it to the hallway, Renata deciding it should stand at the very end like a guardian watching over the Grizzly Wing.

Gabe smirked, stepping back to admire their work. "You think the guests will appreciate being stared down by a bear every time they walk through here?"

Renata tilted her chin, grinning. "I prefer to think of it as welcoming them to Montana properly."

The Fishing Wing came together next. Rustic, inviting, a perfect match for the lodge's atmosphere. But Gabe barely noticed the decor now. Only noticed her. How she moved, how she smiled, how she threw herself into making this place feel like home. And something deep inside him clenched. Because it wasn't just about the lodge. It was about her. Her place here. Her place with him.

Renata reached for a framed trout painting, hanging it on the wall, her fingers lingering against the glass longer than necessary. Gabe watched, catching the slight furrow in her brow, the way she swiped her thumb once over the corner of the frame, as if steadying herself.

Then she turned, catching him staring. Gabe didn't look away. Didn't pretend he wasn't watching her like a man, completely, utterly gone for her. Her lips parted, like she might say something. But then she blinked, gripped the frame just a little tighter, then let go, stepping back, shaking her head slightly, breaking the spell.

Gabe clenched his jaw, letting out a slow breath. Yeah. He was in deep. The thought of her leaving sat heavy in his chest, unbearable in a way he hadn't fully processed yet.

As they stepped outside, Renata stretched her arms, exhaling. For now, she looked lighter. But Gabe wasn't fooled. He could see it. The way she wasn't letting herself hold the joy for too long, the way something still lingered in her mind. And he wanted to know what it was. Wanted to fix it, carry it, take whatever was weighing her down and lift it right off her shoulders. But he couldn't. Not yet. Not until she let him in.

So instead, he turned toward the truck, grabbing the last box of frames. "We still need a theme for the second floor," he said casually, nudging her back into lodge-planning mode.

Renata exhaled slowly, pausing. He could see her trying to regain her enthusiasm. "Big Sky Rooms," she said confidently. "And Timberline Rooms."

Gabe smirked. "Sounds perfect."

And just like that, for now, she let herself enjoy the moment again. But Gabe wouldn't forget. Wouldn't forget the way her joy had dimmed so fast, how she'd snapped back into silence right after that call. Wouldn't forget that whatever was bothering her mattered. And mattered more than she wanted to admit. And if it mattered to her, it mattered to him.

16

RENATA SAT AT the Braxton family's dinner table, listening to the soft murmur of conversation and the occasional clatter of dishes. The long day of yard sales and decorating the lodge had exhausted her body, but her mind wouldn't settle. She should feel content. She was surrounded by people who had welcomed her in. Haydon shaking her head at Gabe's latest half-serious argument with Harlan, a smirk tugging at the corner of her mouth as she let them banter. Harlan grinned, stretching the truth with every detail of his wild cow-chasing adventure that morning, while Gabe leaned back, arms crossed, listening with exaggerated skepticism.

The warmth of this house, the steadiness of this family, filled her up in a way she didn't want to leave behind. And yet... Dalton's ultimatum. The life waiting for her back in Arizona. The life here, pulling at her in ways she hadn't expected.

She should tell them. Should say something to Gabe, to his family, to anyone who could give her an answer she wasn't sure she could find on her own. But she couldn't bring herself to ruin the moment. Her cousin's words loomed over her like a storm cloud. Tomorrow. She had to decide tomorrow. Stay. Or go.

Her fork hovered over her plate. She pressed her fingertips against the cool metal, grounding herself, but it didn't stop the tightening in her chest. She forced herself to take a bite, but the food blurred on her plate. Tomorrow swallowed everything else.

A quiet movement beside her made her glance up. Gabe. Not speaking, not pushing, just watching, just noticing. His brow furrowed slightly, the smallest flicker of concern passing through his silver-blue eyes before he turned back to Haydon's teasing. She exhaled slowly, willing herself to hold on to this moment. Tomorrow could wait.

She picked up her plate and carried it to the kitchen, the familiar routine settling around her like a shield against what was coming. Loading the dishwasher, stacking cups, clearing off the table. One simple task after another. Until finally, she ran out of things to do.

Renata turned toward Haydon, forcing a lightness into her voice. "Hey, want to see the lodge?"

Harlan's eyes lit up, his fork clattering against his plate as he sat up straighter. "Yeah!"

So, once everything was cleaned up, Renata met them at the lodge. Harlan's excitement burst open the moment they walked inside, and he darted down the Fishing Wing, calling for Gabe to follow. Renata let out a breath, adjusting the brim of her hat, then turned to Haydon. If she could just focus on this, maybe she wouldn't have to think about tomorrow.

She led her deeper inside, her voice steady, her hands gesturing naturally, as if she weren't giving a farewell tour to the place she loved more than she had words for. "This is the check-in area." Renata motioned toward the front desk, the flower arrangement adding a quiet softness, the framed welcome sign giving warmth to the space. Things she made herself with the front desk in mind.

Haydon nodded, running a hand over the counter's polished surface. "Feels inviting."

Renata swallowed, forcing a smile. "That's the goal."

They made their way down the hall, passing the massive

stone fireplace, its mantle now holding framed photographs of images she had taken, images of the Broken Spur's pastures, its barns, its quiet beauty. Haydon's gaze swept over every detail. She wasn't just looking. She was seeing.

"It's welcoming. Beautiful." Haydon murmured, fingertips brushing over the carved wood. "You're becoming a part of this place."

Renata froze. Opened her mouth. Closed it. She pushed forward instead. As if moving faster could outrun the weight pressing into her ribs.

Renata stepped into the next room, gesturing toward the framed photographs of Montana's thick forests, their rich greens blending seamlessly with the deep wood tones. "This is the Timberline Wing," she said, running a hand along the edge of a carved wooden lamp, its design mimicking tree rings. "Wanted to make it feel like the forest."

Haydon nodded, slow and thoughtful. Her gaze lingered, not just admiring, but remembering. She exhaled quietly. "Vern would've loved this."

Renata blinked, caught off guard. She hadn't expected that. "Yeah? Do you think this matches his vision for the lodge?"

Haydon's lips tilted in a knowing, bittersweet way. "He always said places should feel like they belong to the land, not just sit on top of it. This. This belongs."

Renata pressed her lips together, suddenly aware of the weight pressing against her ribs, tight and unrelenting. Haydon turned toward her, eyes steady. "You've done something good here, Renata." She nodded toward the surrounding space. "Something that matters."

Renata swallowed. She wanted to believe that. But did she really? Or was she just trying to make this place feel more like hers because deep down, she already knew she wanted to stay?

She forced a breath, stepping into another room, her voice straining despite her efforts to sound normal. "This," she said, her voice tighter, her breath shallower, "is the Grizzly Wing."

The deep brown tones, carved bear figurines on the nightstands, the massive framed images of grizzlies midstride or peering from behind trees. It was all exactly how she envisioned it. She ran her fingers along the edge of a carved bear, tracing its features absently, as if touching it could steady her thoughts.

Haydon stood in the doorway. Watching. Waiting. Renata's throat tightened. She blinked fast, searching for something, anything, to hold her together. She reached for one of the framed images, adjusting it even though it was perfectly straight. A stall. A distraction.

And then it was too much. The lump in her throat became unbearable. Her hands gripped the edge of the nightstand before she could stop herself. She inhaled sharply. And broke.

Renata sank onto the edge of the bed, curling her fingers into the thick quilt beneath her, trying to breathe through the ache lodged deep in her chest. "I don't want to leave."

The words slipped out, raw and unfiltered, cracking at the edges. Haydon stood near the door for a beat, then stepped inside, closing it behind her. Giving Renata space. Giving her privacy.

"Tell me," Haydon said quietly, sitting beside her.

Renata exhaled, shaking her head. "My cousin gave me an ultimatum. I have to decide by tomorrow."

Haydon didn't react, not in shock, not in immediate advice. Just listened. Renata pressed her palms against her thighs, staring at the floor. "I love Montana. I love the lodge. I love what we're building here. It feels right. It feels..."

She hesitated. Her pulse tapped hard against her temple. It felt like Gabe. And her. The thought formed before she could push it away. She didn't say it aloud. Didn't have to. Haydon simply watched her, patient and steady.

Renata inhaled sharply. "But if I stay, I'm walking away

from everything I've ever known. My family's business, my job, my life in Arizona. My parents. My sister. How do I just… let that go?"

Haydon took a slow breath, her gaze settling on the framed grizzly print on the wall, then back on Renata. "You know Ross grew up here," she said, voice measured. "Montana ran in his blood. Wide-open spaces, cold winters. This ranch. It was all he ever knew."

Renata swallowed, nodding. "But then God led him somewhere new. Arizona. A place he never expected to love, but now? He wouldn't trade it for anything."

Haydon turned toward her fully, her voice quiet but sure. "God doesn't always keep us where we start, Renata. Sometimes He calls us somewhere new. And sometimes, He makes our hearts ready for it long before we realize."

Renata blinked fast. Her mind turned over Haydon's words, settling deep into something she couldn't shake. Maybe, just maybe, God had already been leading her away from Arizona long before she ever considered leaving. She thought about the surrogacy. Leaving to escape the pain. Then how Montana had tugged at her in ways she hadn't expected.

Had this always been the plan? Had she just been slow to see it? Her breath hitched slightly. She had spent so much time carrying responsibilities, expectations, and obligations that she had never considered choosing her own path. Finding a new home in a new place. But now she could. And she would.

A slow, certain breath moved through her, filling the space inside her chest that had felt so uncertain for so long. She was choosing this place. Choosing this life. And choosing the man who had quietly stolen her heart, piece by piece, when she wasn't looking.

GABE FOLLOWED AFTER Harlan, listening with half an ear as his nephew took in the lodge with wide-eyed enthusiasm. "This place is sick," Harlan declared, running his fingers over the carved trout sitting on a bookshelf.

Gabe smirked. "Sick, huh?"

"Yeah." Harlan nodded, completely serious. "Like, old-school cool. Not boring-old-school. Good-old-school."

Gabe chuckled, shaking his head. "That's high praise, kid."

Harlan grinned and darted ahead, Gabe trailing behind. Or at least, that's what he was supposed to be doing. But his mind wasn't here. It was on her. Renata. Something had been off at dinner. Not obvious, not dramatic, but there, lingering beneath the surface. A quietness. A weight.

He had caught her looking at him once or twice, a flicker of something unreadable in her expression. Not avoidance, but restraint. Like she was holding something back.

Before Gabe could dwell too long on it, he turned the corner, and froze. Haydon stood in the hallway, arms wrapped around Renata, holding her in a firm hug. And Renata... Her eyes were red. His stomach dropped. Something had happened. Something big.

Before he could think better of it, he closed the space between them. Haydon pulled back first, giving Renata one last squeeze before turning to Gabe.

"Keys," she said, holding out a hand. "I'm taking Harlan home. Think Renata can drop you off whenever?"

Gabe barely nodded, fishing his keys from his pocket and handing them over. Haydon gave him one last knowing look before she and Harlan slipped out the door. And then she was gone.

Now, it was just them. Just him. And her. Standing there, looking too small, too vulnerable for the fierce woman he knew.

Gabe hesitated, but the words came instinctively.

"What's wrong?"

Renata exhaled, fingers tightening slightly against her arms, a quiet brace against what she was about to say. "Dalton called."

His stomach plunged. A cold weight settled deep inside him. Of course. Of course, Dalton had called. Pushing for her decision, pulling her back toward Arizona, toward the life she had always known.

"Yeah?" Gabe forced the word out, even though his pulse had already picked up.

She ran a hand through her hair, her breath measured, but heavier now. "He wants me back," she admitted. "Vacation's over, and he needs me at the resort. I built that role, trained the staff, ran the resort. He's ready for me to step back in."

Gabe swallowed hard. He had known this was coming. Knew Dalton had been waiting for her to come back and resume the job that had always been hers. And he knew, because he had learned under her at Vargas Guest Ranch & Resort, had watched her run that place seamlessly, had seen firsthand how effortlessly she owned that world.

It was her career. Her life. Her family. Montana was only ever supposed to be temporary. A break. A respite. A place for her to heal. He knew that. And he fell in love with her, anyway. And now, she had to decide whether to go back to it.

Gabe forced his voice to stay steady. "And?"

Renata met his gaze. A beat of silence stretched between them. Then, she said firmly, "I want to stay."

Relief crashed into him like a wave, like air rushing back into his lungs after drowning. "I need to move to town," she continued, her voice sharpening with quiet determination. "Find a place. Get a job. Figure out how to make this work."

His brain scrambled to catch up. She was staying. But she was leaving the ranch. Not staying here. Not staying with him. That wasn't okay. That wasn't what he wanted.

The words slipped out before he could stop them. "Work for me."

Renata stilled. "What?"

His pulse pounded loudly in his ears, drowning out any common sense. He swallowed. "Be the guest ranch manager. Help run the lodge."

She blinked. Processing. Weighing. Considering. Please, God, let her say yes.

"I—I don't know," she admitted slowly, her brow furrowing slightly. "I never even thought about that."

Of course, she hadn't. Because she had been thinking about leaving the ranch, moving away, making her own way. And that was the last thing Gabe wanted.

"You really think that's a good idea?" she asked, watching him closely, sharp and perceptive.

"Yes," he said. Too fast. Too sure. Because it was.

Renata let out a breath, studying him. "I'll think about it."

She glanced away, pressing her lips together as if trying to steady herself. Gabe nodded, even though it wasn't the answer he wanted. Silence settled between them, not tense, but heavy. Full of everything they weren't saying.

She squared her shoulders, then reached for her purse. He realized, in that quiet motion, that their conversation had ended, but the uncertainty hadn't. "Let's go," she murmured, turning toward the door.

Gabe followed, stepping outside with her, the crisp Montana air wrapping around them. It wasn't until they climbed into the truck that he let out a breath he didn't realize he'd been holding.

The drive back to the ranch was quiet. Too quiet. The truck rumbled as Renata pulled up to the ranch house, the headlights sweeping across the porch, illuminating the very place he already imagined her walking in and out of every day.

She could stay. She could be here. She could be his, if he

could make this work. Gabe hesitated before opening the door, stealing one last glance at her.

"See you tomorrow?"

Renata met his gaze, something unreadable flickering behind her eyes. "Yeah."

And then she was gone. The truck's taillights faded down the drive, disappearing into the night. Gabe let out a slow, uneven breath, staring at the empty space where she had been.

She was staying. But he had no idea how he was going to make it work. Fear settled deep. He had just made the biggest offer of his life, one he had no certainty he could deliver on. But losing her wasn't an option. So somehow, he would make this happen.

17

———————

RENATA SAT ON the sofa, staring out at the scenic Montana mountains in the distance, phone in hand. She'd waited until now on purpose. Sunday family dinner would be over by now. Plates scraped clean, laughter lingering in the kitchen, her parents still seated at the dining table, talking about work and life with her cousins and their spouses.

She could almost hear it. Aunt Catalina reminding everyone they needed to eat more, her mom stealing an extra empanada, Solana's joyous laughter mixing in with the others. She missed them. She missed all of it. The rhythm, the warmth, the familiarity of being surrounded by the people she'd known her whole life.

For a fleeting moment, she could see herself there, sitting in her usual seat, passing dishes across the table. Watching Cliff crawl onto Raina's lap—his mother's lap. Peace settled over her at the image of the baby she had carried for nine months rightfully in the arms of his mother and father.

She had done what God had called her to. To be a safe place for Cliff to grow and come into the world. Nothing more. Her chest tightened, but the feeling wasn't doubt. It was love. A love that didn't mean she had heard God's calling wrong. It was okay for her to love Cliff far deeper than any of her other cousins' children. It was okay for her to have a special bond with him and then for her to let go.

And just because that love hurt, that she would always

miss him in a way no one could ever truly understand, didn't mean she'd gotten it wrong. Suddenly, she felt a profound sense of rightness about it all. Carrying Cliff. Giving birth to him. Handing him to his rightful, loving, biological parents. Coming to Montana. Helping Gabe. Working for Gabe. It was all right. All God's plan for her life.

1 Peter 1:6-7 came to mind. You rejoice in this, even though now for a short time, if necessary, you suffer grief in various trials so that the proven character of your faith, more valuable than gold which, though perishable, is refined by fire—may result in praise, glory, and honor at the revelation of Jesus Christ.

Part of God's plan for her included testing her faith. Testing her character. Refining her through the experience, like those verses said, so that it would bring praise, glory, and honor to Jesus. Cliff being born brought Jesus honor. Giving Raina and Devon the gift of a biological child brought glory to Jesus. Helping Gabe felt like another part of God's plan, like she was meant to be here, meant to help, meant to stay.

And even though she missed her family and loved them fiercely, it didn't mean she had to go back. Montana was her future, was God's plan for her life.

Renata sighed and shifted her gaze to her phone, pulling up Dalton's contact. She had rehearsed the conversation with him a dozen times in her head, but now that she was about to make the call, her throat felt tight, her thoughts tangled. Still, she knew what she had to say.

Exhaling slowly, she pressed the call button. Dalton answered after only a couple of rings, his expression expectant but not impatient. He was waiting for her answer. They both knew it.

"Hey," she said, willing her voice to stay steady, even as faint laughter from family dinner echoed behind him.

"Hey yourself," he replied, the warmth of the background noise fading as he moved into his office. "So. Have you thought about it?"

The breath she took wasn't quite deep enough to stop the ache in her chest. "I have." She paused. "I'm staying in Montana."

Dalton didn't react immediately, but she caught the slight raise of his eyebrows, the way his jaw tightened almost imperceptibly. "Okay," he said, measured, unreadable. "You're sure?"

She nodded. "Yeah. I am."

Silence stretched, but it wasn't uncomfortable. "I figured this might be your answer," he finally admitted. "Still feels weird, you leaving Vargas Ranch behind."

"I'm not rejecting anything as I leave," she said softly. "I'm... choosing something new. God's plan for my life."

Dalton let out a slow breath, then nodded. She knew this wasn't the answer he wanted, but he wasn't going to fight her on it. "I'll handle things here," he said. "The resort will be fine."

She smiled, grateful. "Thanks, Dalton. For everything."

"Yeah, yeah," he muttered, shaking his head but with the ghost of a smile. "Guess I'll see you around, Montana cuz."

The nickname made her chest squeeze, but for the first time, it wasn't painful. It was right. She hung up before the emotion could take over completely, staring at the blank screen for a long moment. The finality of it settled over her. Not heavy, not suffocating, but anchoring. She had made her choice. And it wasn't just about staying in Montana. It was about trusting that God had led her here for a reason. Maybe for many reasons.

A deep breath eased out of her, slow and sure. Her gaze drifted toward the window, toward the mountains stretching vast and certain in the fading afternoon light. Her home. Her future.

Her phone buzzed lightly in her hand, pulling her attention back. Solana. Renata exhaled, adjusted her grip, then tapped the video call button before settling deeper into the couch.

It only took a few moments before Solana's face popped onto the screen, bright, familiar, and full of warmth. "Finally!" Solana grinned, leaning back against the pillows. "I was wondering when my sister was gonna stop avoiding me."

Renata exhaled a soft laugh. "I wasn't avoiding you."

Solana arched a brow. "Mm-hmm. Sure."

Renata smiled, but didn't argue. Maybe part of her had been avoiding this moment, the conversation they needed to have, the emotions they needed to untangle. But now she was ready.

"I made my decision," Renata said, carefully, but with certainty.

Solana's expression changed subtly, interest sparking in her eyes. "About Montana?"

Renata nodded. "I'm staying."

For a beat, Solana didn't react. "Wow. Montana must be really nice."

Renata rolled her eyes. Solana smirked. "I mean, I get it. I hear there's a certain very handsome cowboy you've been helping out..."

Renata groaned. "Really? That's where your mind goes first?"

She wasn't wrong. Gabe was a part of her decision. Solana laughed, but her expression softened. "I'm happy for you, Rennie. I really am."

Renata swallowed. She wasn't sure how much she needed to hear that until this very moment. "I feel like it's God's plan for me," she admitted. "Even though it's scary, even though I miss home... I miss you."

Solana's smile dimmed slightly as she grew misty-eyed. "I miss you too."

A few seconds passed before Renata spoke again, gentler this time. "Why didn't you tell me?"

Solana blinked. "Tell you what?"

Renata didn't waver. "About the baby."

Solana hesitated, biting her lower lip as her brow furrowed. She let out a slow breath and her shoulders dropped. "I didn't want to make things worse for you."

Renata's chest tightened. Solana kept going, voice softer. "You went through so much with Cliff... I just thought if I told you I was pregnant, it would hurt."

Renata inhaled deeply, absorbing the weight of those words. "Solana... I want to share in your joys. And in your sorrows. That's never changed."

Solana's eyes reddened with unshed tears. "I just didn't want to be the reason you felt more grief."

Renata shook her head. "You're not. And you never will be."

For a moment, Solana didn't speak. But then her expression melted into something vulnerable, something unguarded. "I love you, Rennie."

Renata's voice wavered slightly. "I love you, too."

Renata lowered the phone slowly, the screen going dark in her hands. The conversation lingered, Solana's joy, her reassurance, the undeniable warmth of their sisterhood, despite the miles between them. And beneath it all, peace settled deep in her chest.

She had made her choice. And for the first time, there was no wavering, no lingering doubt. She was staying. Her gaze drifted toward the window, where the Montana mountains stretched vast and endless in the fading afternoon light. She loved this place. She loved the quiet, the land, the work she had found herself pouring into. And she loved the people who had made it feel like home.

Her phone buzzed. Gabe. *You up for a day off tomorrow? I've got a surprise for you.*

Renata's heart kicked a little harder than it should have, warmth unfurling through her chest. She hesitated only a second before typing back. *See you tomorrow.*

Almost without thinking, she added: *Looking forward to*

it.

A small smile tugged at her lips as she set the phone down. She was home. And for the first time, she let herself be excited about everything and everyone waiting for her here.

GABE LEANED AGAINST the stall door, eyes fixed on the calf as she stirred in the straw. She had grown. Stronger. Surer. Ready. And yet, he knew the day she was fully weaned would still feel like a loss, a severing of something that had been there since the moment she took her first breath.

His stomach tightened. Renata was severing something, too. Not just her job, not just her home, but her family. Sunday family dinner. The chaotic, joyful rhythm of a home filled with parents, cousins, nieces, nephews, laughter. She was leaving behind people who had always known her, always loved her. For him. For herself.

And he had to make Montana worth it, not just in some vague, hopeful way, but in a way that made her never doubt that she had made the right choice. But finances were tight. Too tight.

He exhaled sharply, dragging a hand over his face, then turned at the sound of footsteps. Haydon leaned against the stall, arms crossed, watching him with the kind of amused scrutiny only a sister could pull off.

"You have been standing here brooding for a solid five minutes," she noted. "Gotta say it's a new look for you."

Gabe huffed. "Not brooding."

Haydon smirked. "Right. Just deeply contemplating life over a calf."

He shot her a look, but she wasn't wrong. Before he could deflect, she tipped her head slightly. "It's about her, isn't it?"

Gabe sighed, rubbing at the back of his neck. "She's staying," he admitted. "But..."

"But you don't know how to make it work."

His silence was answer enough. Haydon pushed off the stall, stepping closer. "Gabe. Tell me exactly how much thought you gave to offering Renata that job before the words left your mouth."

His jaw ticked. "I..." She arched a brow. "None," he admitted flatly, his gut twisting, anticipating a reprimand.

Haydon sighed, shaking her head, but not unkindly. "You love her," she said simply.

She didn't phrase it as a question. Because it wasn't. The words slammed into him, clean, direct, irreversible. His pulse kicked hard, a reaction he barely contained. Love. It wasn't that he hadn't felt it. Hadn't known it in some deep, unspoken part of himself. But saying it aloud? That made it real. That made it something he couldn't take back.

A breath lodged in his throat, a split-second moment where his instincts screamed at him to deflect, to brush it off, to protect himself from everything that came with admitting it. But he couldn't. Not to Haydon. Not when it was the truth.

He swallowed hard. "Yeah."

"Yeah," Haydon echoed, watching him carefully. "And you were desperate to keep her here."

It wasn't judgment, just understanding. Still, it stung. Because she was right. "She's worth it," he murmured, almost to himself.

Haydon exhaled, nudging his arm again, firmer this time. "Come on. Let's go look at the numbers."

Gabe lingered for a moment, his gaze drifting back to the calf. She was strong, sure, ready for whatever came next. Just like Renata. He exhaled, then pushed off the stall, following Haydon toward the house.

The barn door creaked as they stepped into the crisp

evening air, the weight of the conversation settling deeper in his chest. The lodge lights glowed warmly from its perch, overlooking the pond, cutting through the growing dusk. Renata's new home. His home. He had to make it work. Had to make this place something she'd never regret choosing.

Haydon pulled open the door, the scent of coffee lingering in the air. She headed straight for the dining room, dropping into her usual seat and cracking open the laptop. "Alright, little brother," she said, fingers already flying over the keyboard. "Let's figure out how to make this job actually work."

Gabe sat at the dining room table, arms crossed, scanning the spreadsheet in front of him. Numbers. Too many numbers. And none of them looked good. Haydon sat across from him, her expression focused, calculating, her fingers flying over the keyboard as she adjusted figures.

After another moment, she leaned back, tapping the final number on the screen. "This," she said, "is what we can afford."

Gabe exhaled sharply, staring at the number. A salary. Barely enough to get by. "And we can offer her room and board. But not in the yurt. We need the income from it."

"I don't think we should give her Ross's room." Way too close to his. Too tempting.

Haydon screwed up her face. "Vern planned for the 'what if we hire someone' scenario. When the lodge was built, he had the architect design a private living space just off the office, intended for the manager."

Haydon tapped the screen. "So with all those caveats, this is what we can afford."

His gut twisted. Renata could make twice this—three times this—if she went back to Arizona. His voice came out rough, quiet. "I hope it's enough."

Haydon didn't even blink. "It is."

Gabe looked up. "Is it?"

Haydon leaned forward, resting her elbows on the table.

"She's not staying for the paycheck, Gabe."

The words hit him, cutting through every excuse, every worry, every single doubt he had been clinging to. "She's staying for you."

A breath lodged in his throat. He gripped the edge of the dining room table like a lifeline. It was different hearing it out loud, not just assuming, not just hoping, but knowing. He swallowed hard, staring at the spreadsheet, seeing nothing but that truth. She was staying. For him. For Montana. For herself.

Haydon sat back, watching him carefully, then smirked. "Well," she drawled, "since you're no longer spiraling, why don't you take the day off tomorrow?"

Gabe blinked. "What?"

She shrugged. "Spend time with Renata. Woo her. Hard launch it if you're feeling bold."

Gabe snorted. "Define the relationship?"

She grinned. "What do you have to lose?"

Gabe held her gaze for a second, then exhaled roughly. Only everything. She tapped the screen again, drawing his attention back. "You need to show her why she's staying."

His chest tightened again, but this time, it wasn't panic. It was a certainty. Haydon stood, stretching. "Take her on a ride. Flathead Lake. Can't go wrong with a view like that."

Gabe stared at her, then exhaled slowly. "She'd like that."

Haydon smirked, heading toward the kitchen. "Good. Then go make it happen."

Gabe scrubbed a hand over his face, leaning back in his chair as Haydon disappeared into the kitchen. The conversation had settled things, at least on paper. Numbers, logistics, a plan. But none of it silenced the unease still twisting in his gut. None of it answered the deeper questions, the ones no spreadsheet could solve.

He pushed up from the table, exhaling sharply as he padded to the stairs, his footsteps quieter than usual. By the time he reached his room, the exhaustion had fully settled, not just from the day, but from the weight of everything pressing on his chest.

His fingers hovered over the doorknob, tightening, then loosening. A slow breath in. Then he exhaled sharply, dragging a hand through his hair before turning the knob and stepping inside. His gaze flicked to the worn easy chair in the corner, the same one he'd collapsed into so many nights before, seeking silence, seeking clarity, seeking something beyond his own tangled thoughts. Tonight was no different.

He dropped into the chair, elbows on his knees, and let out a slow breath. Then, finally, he did what he should have done hours ago. He prayed, softly at first.

"Lord."

The word sat heavy in the quiet room, more weighted than any thought that had passed through his mind today. He swallowed. "I should have come to You first. Should have trusted You more than my own desperation."

The truth of it settled deep, the moment Renata said she was staying, he had focused on fixing things himself, instead of handing them over to the One who actually could. His fingers tightened around each other. "I don't know what You have planned," he admitted. "But I need Your wisdom. Not just for the ranch. For Renata. For me."

He sighed, the weight pressing deeper into his chest, then slowly released it. "I pray for her," he murmured. "For her conversation with Dalton. For her heart as she chooses this new life. For her peace in leaving everything behind."

A pause. His throat tightened slightly. "And if—if this thing between us is meant to be... if I'm meant to be the man she chooses..." He swallowed. "Let it be right. Let it be Your plan, not just mine."

The quiet deepened, wrapping around him like a solid, steady presence. "I pray for the ranch. For the finances. For every decision I have to make." His grip loosened, submission replacing the strain. "And I trust You. Even when I don't see the answers. Even when I don't know how this all works out."

He let out a slow breath, feeling the weight lifting. Not gone, but carried. Then, softly, honestly, he whispered, "I sure hope Renata's part of it."

18

THE MORNING FELT different. Maybe it was the weight of everything that had settled after last night, the conversation with Haydon, the prayer, the decision to just... trust. Or maybe it was because today wasn't about thinking. It was about doing.

Gabe cinched the saddle straps, pulling them taut with a practiced motion, the leather creaking softly beneath his grip. The scent of oiled tack and sun-warmed hay filled the barn, mingling with the earthy musk of the horses, their quiet breath puffing in the cool morning air.

He wasn't nervous. At least, that's what he kept telling himself. But the subtle tension in his shoulders, the way he adjusted the stirrups twice when they didn't need adjusting, said otherwise. He shouldn't be overthinking this. It was just a ride. A simple, peaceful ride. But everything about today felt heavier, like the weight of something unspoken lingered in the dust motes drifting through the barn's slatted sunlight.

Gabe ran a hand along his horse's neck, his palm brushing over the warm, familiar roughness of the animal's coat, then exhaled slowly. She'd be here any second. And he needed this day to be good.

He glanced up as Renata stepped into the barn, sunlight catching in her dark brown cowgirl hat, casting a soft shadow over her face. His breath hitched, just slightly. She looked like an authentic Montana cowgirl. Her fitted jeans, worn cowgirl boots, and flowered snap-front shirt gave her an authentic western flair she hadn't had when they met, casual yet striking against her caramel skin.

Not in Arizona. Back then, she had been eight months pregnant, sitting in her office, wearing a rust-colored maternity dress that flowed over her swollen belly, soft and understated. A dress. Something he never thought he'd remember so vividly, but the detail had seared itself into his mind. Like so many things about his formerly pregnant cowgirl.

And now? Now, she was thin again, her baby weight long gone, her presence just as steady. But different, too. She wasn't just passing through Montana anymore. She was part of it.

"You ready?" he asked, voice steady, but barely.

She nodded, a smile playing at the edges of her lips. "Think so."

They rode in quiet, the crisp air wrapping around them cool and fresh, like the first breath after rain. Tall pine trees stretched high overhead, their scent rich and earthy, mixing with the whisper of a breeze swirling through the branches. Above them, the vast sky was littered with white puffy clouds drifting lazily against the deep blue. A perfect day for a ride. And Gabe couldn't wait to see her face when they reached the lake overlook.

Every mile closer, his anticipation twisted tighter. She rode confidently beside him, her posture loose, comfortable. Like she belonged here. And then they crested the ridge and the pine trees parted, revealing the deep blue, stunning, unmoving Flathead Lake in its quiet strength.

Renata pulled her horse to a stop beside him, breath catching slightly. "It's incredible," she murmured, eyes locked on the water.

Gabe swallowed, his pulse kicking once, hard. This was the moment. "I wanted to bring you here because Montana has things like this," he said, voice quieter now. "Things that remind you why you stay."

Her gaze flicked to him, curious, waiting. He exhaled slowly. "I want you to stay," he admitted. "And not just for me. For yourself. Because this place is home for you now."

She said nothing, just watched him, waiting. "So," he continued, "I want to offer you something official. A job. Here. At the lodge."

A beat. She absorbed it. Then a slow smile tugged at her lips. "So it's not just a pity job, huh?"

His breath huffed out, amused. "No. It's an actual job. With a real salary."

He named the pathetically meagre amount before telling her about the room and board. "And it's yours if you want it."

Her fingers ran lightly over her reins, gaze drifting back toward the lake. Then, without hesitation. "I want it."

Gabe blinked, something warm unfurling in his chest. "You sure?"

She looked at him then, really looked at him, and nodded. "I'm sure."

She was sure. The tightness in his chest eased, not gone, but lighter now, steadier. For weeks, he'd wrestled with this, keeping her here, giving her reasons to stay that went beyond him. And yet, looking at her now, bathed in Montana's golden sunlight, her gaze unwavering, he realized she had already chosen this life long before he put it into words.

It was never about convincing her. It was about accepting that she already belonged here. Gabe let out a slow breath, giving her a quiet nod. "Good."

SHE WOULD HAVE said yes even if the job came with a cheap tent in the middle of winter. The salary? It didn't matter. Because Renata wouldn't have to leave the Broken Spur. She wouldn't have to leave Gabe. Her fingers tightened slightly around the reins as the weight of that thought settled in her chest.

Because this wasn't just about staying in Montana. It was about staying with Gabe. She looked over at him, taking him in. The soft wear of his flannel stretched over broad shoulders, the comfortable way his jeans hung on his frame, the scuffed leather of his boots dusted from the trail.

He looked just like he had the day she met him. Gruff. Uncomfortable. Unshaven, like he hadn't decided whether he cared enough to clean up before stepping into her office in Arizona. She hadn't known what to make of him then. A quiet, sharp-eyed rancher with too many burdens and too few words.

But behind that exterior? Behind the tension in his jaw, the hesitation in his shoulders? There was a kind, thoughtful protector. A man who had helped her through the darkest season of her life, never asking for anything in return. A man who had eased her emotional burden and given her space to heal when she didn't even know what healing looked like.

And somehow, despite everything that could have made them complicated, he had shown tremendous restraint, if their almost-kisses were any sign. And she loved it. Loved helping him build this place, loved watching him work, loved seeing the lodge come together piece by piece, knowing they had built it side by side.

So, yeah. She would have said yes without pay. Renata exhaled, letting the weight of her decision settle in. She had a job here. A purpose. A place. More than that, she had Gabe. The certainty of it hummed beneath her skin, steady and sure.

Gabe cleared his throat, shifting in the saddle, his gaze flicking between her and the lake. "Well," he murmured, nudging his horse forward, voice just a touch gruff, "since you're officially a Montana resident now, I think that calls for lunch."

Renata laughed, following him down toward the shaded clearing just beyond the ridge. Pine and lake water scented the air, the breeze catching her hair as they rode. A new closeness passed between them, unspoken but real.

When they reached the clearing, Gabe swung off his horse with practiced ease, boots pressing into the soft grass. Then his hand extended toward her. She took it. No hesitation. And maybe it was nothing, or maybe it was everything. The reassuring pressure of his hand, a silent promise of stability she had always relied on.

Gabe spread out a blanket in the sun with a boulder behind them. As they settled onto the blanket, the spread wasn't fancy. Just ham sandwiches, chips, and a thermos of unsweetened tea. But it was exactly right. And for the first time in weeks, she could just breathe.

Gabe handed her a sandwich, then leaned back against the boulder, studying her for a moment. "You seem lighter," he observed, biting off a corner of his sandwich.

Renata smiled, staring down at her tea, then nodded. "I feel lighter."

A pause. Softly she said, "I prayed last night."

Gabe's gaze flicked to her. Her fingers tightened slightly around her cup. "Not just for the ranch. For myself. For clarity."

Gabe exhaled, nodding slowly, as if he understood exactly what she meant. "Me too," he admitted.

She glanced at him, waiting. He sighed, rubbing a hand over his face, fingers pressing briefly against his brow before falling away. "For so long, I kept trying to fix everything. Keep the ranch afloat. Make sure you had reasons to stay. Make sure the ranch could handle it."

Renata's heart hitched, just slightly. She knew he had worried about her leaving. But she hadn't realized how deeply he had carried that fear. His voice softened. "But I realized last night that I can't control any of it. I just had to let go. Give it to God."

A quiet warmth settled between them. Renata swallowed, letting his words sink in. She had fought herself. Her fear, her hesitation, her instinct to run. And she had found peace in surrendering it. Just like Gabe had.

Her voice was quieter now. "I realized something too."

He lifted a brow, waiting. She exhaled, gaze fixed on the lake. At this distance, the large boat seemed tiny, its wake hardly noticeable. "I used to think faith meant knowing everything. Having clarity before making a choice. And once making the choice, if it was truly from God, there wouldn't be pain." She shook her head. "But it doesn't work that way, does it?"

Gabe didn't answer right away. A few seconds ticked by before he finally said, "No. It means stepping forward anyway. Trusting Him in all things. The pain. The joy."

Her breath caught. Because that was it. That was the lesson they had both learned. And that was exactly what she was choosing now.

Gabe chewed a bite before tossing her a smirk. "You know, if we were real professionals, we'd have packed something fancier than ham sandwiches."

She scoffed. "Please. Like anything beats a good ham sandwich."

His laugh was low, warm, deep enough to settle something inside her. The conversation moved easily. Catching up, teasing, talking about the grand opening, the last few days, the call with Dalton and Solana.

And somewhere in the pauses between words, a subtle changed happened. Gabe was watching her now. Not like before, not with hesitation, but with quiet understanding. And Renata felt it, too. Everything they had walked through, everything they had built here. It wasn't just in the past. It was part of her now, part of them.

Renata exhaled, heart beating steadier now. "I love you, Gabe."

The words fell from her lips before she even thought to second-guess them. Because she did. She had for a while. Maybe not in ways she had fully admitted to herself. But she knew it now. And she wasn't afraid to say it.

For a beat, Gabe just looked at her. Not in shock, not in hesitation, but as if taking her words into his heart. Then, with a husky timbre, he whispered, "I love you, Rennie. So much."

Renata felt the pause, the barest breath of space between them, the moment where he didn't rush, didn't hesitate. Just looked at her, taking her in completely, as if memorizing every flicker of emotion in her eyes, the soft rise of her breath, the way her lips parted slightly in anticipation.

And then warmth. His hand rose, cradling her jaw, thumb tracing the curve of her cheekbone before sliding lower, rough fingers skimming the sensitive hollow of her neck. A shiver ran through her, not from the cold, not from nerves, but from the undeniable depth of the moment, the way his touch held unspoken meaning, steady and sure.

Then, finally, his lips met hers. Slow. Certain. A promise. The kiss deepened, heat unfurling between them, his fingers threading gently into her hair, anchoring her to him. Her hand resting against his clean-shaven jaw. And she kissed him back without hesitation, without second-guessing, with nothing left between them but absolute trust.

This was right. This was joy. He was her home.

Renata melted into Gabe's hold, the warmth of his kiss still lingering on her lips, still settling deep in her chest. He didn't pull away completely, not yet. Instead, his arm eased around her, solid and sure, as he gently angled her back toward the view of the lake, keeping her tucked close against his side.

The water stretched before them, its surface rippling gently, reflecting the sky in fluid hues of deep blue and silver, reaching toward the mountains with quiet, timeless grace. And for the first time, she felt like she was a part of it.

Renata exhaled, blinking back into the moment, then frowned slightly. "Wait."

Gabe tilted his head, brow raising, amused. She narrowed her eyes at him. "Did you just call me Rennie?"

The corner of his mouth tugged upward, the beginnings of a quiet, knowing smirk. "Yes. Yes, I did."

Warmth bloomed through her chest from more than just the kiss. From how perfectly he fit. How natural this was, how right. Like pieces falling into place. She let out a soft breath, looking from the lake back to him.

Montana was hers now. The lodge was hers to build alongside him. And in just a few days, the grand opening would mark the beginning of everything they had worked for. She could hardly believe it. A new life. A new future. One that held nothing but possibility and the quiet, unwavering presence of the man beside her.

Renata leaned into him slightly, her fingers brushing over his forearm, then smiled. "Guess I'll have to get used to that."

Gabe's chuckle was low, easy, just rough enough to send warmth curling through her again. "You'd better," he murmured. "Rennie."

She giggled before letting herself sink into the playful truth of his words. Because for the first time in a long time, there was nothing left to doubt. She was exactly where she was supposed to be.

19

GABE HAD NEVER been more aware of the hours passing. Every second carried pressure, tightening across his shoulders, his pulse ticking just a little faster than usual. Guests were arriving slowly at first, trickling in one by one, hesitant yet excited. And he was supposed to look like he knew exactly what he was doing.

He straightened, tilting his head down toward his shoulder, trying to ease the tension in his neck. Then he glanced toward the couple stepping through the entrance, a pair of retirees from Colorado, matching fleece vests and an enthusiasm that made up for their slow gait.

"Welcome to the Broken Spur," Gabe said, offering his best attempt at a steady smile.

The man grinned. "Son, this place is a dream. Look at that view."

He gestured toward the mountains beyond the lodge, their peaks still kissed with snow despite the warmth in the valley. His wife hummed, adjusting her glasses. "The yurts, I saw the gorgeous pictures online, I can't wait to see them. You know, we stayed in one once near Aspen, but it didn't have half the charm this place does."

Charm. That was something Gabe hadn't really considered. He'd been too busy making sure the plumbing worked, and the roads weren't washed out before opening day. Still hearing it now? It settled something in him.

He explained the lodge's amenities, talking as if this wasn't the first time he had ever done this, before guiding them out to their yurt. More guests followed. A young couple from Portland, excited about horseback rides, an older woman from Texas traveling solo, looking for a quiet retreat.

And just when he thought he might be getting the hang of this, Haydon and Harlan appeared, both clearly amused. "Not bad, little brother," Haydon mused, crossing her arms.

Gabe huffed, adjusting his hat. "You here to check my work?"

Harlan grinned. "Nah. Just here to watch you sweat a little."

Gabe sighed, shaking his head, but the teasing grounded him somehow. Reminded him that this was real, that this was happening, that he and Rennie had actually pulled this off.

Then softly, without pretense, Haydon said, "Mom and Dad would be proud of you."

The words hit deep, lodging in his chest. She squeezed his shoulder. "Vern too."

Gabe swallowed, his gaze flicking toward the lodge. Vern would have loved this. Loved Renata. The thought stirred something in his chest. Would he have even met Renata if Vern had still been here? Would his life have ever been shaken enough for her to walk into it?

The truth settled quietly. God had worked this out. The painful parts. The joyous parts. All of it, for this moment. He exhaled slowly.

But before he could dwell too long, the dining hall doors swung open a little too forcefully. One caterer rushed toward him, her face tight with frustration.

"We've got a problem," she said, shaking her head. "The food truck with the afternoon snacks just called — they're delayed. Maybe an hour."

An hour. A full hour of guests expecting food, expecting hospitality, expecting something that was not an empty serving table. Panic itched beneath Gabe's skin.

"An hour?" He ran a hand down his face. "That's—"

"Not a problem," Renata interrupted.

Gabe turned. She stood calm as ever, eyes steady, hands resting lightly on her hips. "I've got this," she assured, then, with that same quiet certainty, she disappeared into the kitchen.

Gabe exhaled, flexing his fingers, trying to tamp down the panic still threading through his ribs. And then the scent hit him. Warm. Rich. Sweet in a way that felt nostalgic.

Renata reappeared, balancing a large tray of fresh-baked cookies, steam curling slightly from their soft centers. Of course, she had baked cookies. He should have known. He should have trusted her more.

Without thinking, he reached for her hand, squeezed her fingers, then leaned in to press a kiss just near the corner of her mouth. A thank-you. A silent promise to do better at trusting her going forward. She let out a soft breath, a flicker of amusement touching her lips.

Gabe barely had time to breathe before another group approached. Five women, all laughing, all unmistakably familiar. He blinked. Blair Everly. And her friends.

She stopped short, her eyes scanning him for half a second before her lips parted in realization. "Wait." Her head tilted slightly. "You're the front desk guy from the resort in Arizona."

Gabe exhaled slowly, rolling his shoulders. "No, Miss Everly." He gave her a measured look, then gestured toward the bustling lodge entrance. "I'm the owner of the Broken Spur. And we're glad to have you and your friends visiting."

Something flashed in Blair's gaze. Surprise, amusement, maybe even a bit of respect. "Huh." She crossed her arms, eyeing him. "Well, look at you, front desk guy turned ranch owner. No wonder you've got things running smoothly."

Renata choked down a laugh, adjusting the tray of cookies in her hands. Blair didn't notice, but one of her friends did. The same blonde friend who had commented on Gabe's looks back in Arizona. She finger-waved at him, her smile slow, interested.

Gabe cleared his throat, shifting slightly. Before anything else could be said, he tossed out casually — "You ladies are checking into Grizzly, right?"

Blair's face twisted in horror. "The bear rooms?" She shook her head sharply. "Oh, absolutely not."

Renata grinned, stepping in smoothly. "They're in Big Sky."

Blair's shoulders settled in immediate relief, but her friend, still watching Gabe with open interest, only smirked knowingly. Then, without hesitation, Gabe reached for Renata's hand. Not dramatic. Not rushed. Just a quiet, unmistakable choice.

And Blair's friend? She clocked the movement instantly. The amusement flickered out of her eyes, replaced with understanding.

"Maybe you should show them to their rooms, Gabe," Renata mused, barely biting back a smile. Then she whispered. "I told you, clean-shaven."

Gabe chuckled, and all his hesitation and nerves fell off his shoulders. He spread his arm in front of him, motioning for the ladies to follow him. "Leave your luggage for a moment and I'll give you the tour before showing you to your rooms."

He winked at Renata and repeated the speech they'd practiced over the last week, highlighting the dining hall, the lobby, and other amenities of their lodge. As Gabe led Blair and her friends through the lobby, weaving through the bustling space, the nerves that had clung to him all morning finally loosened their grip.

The lodge was alive. The guests were settling in. And Renata, she had been right there the whole time, steadying him without needing to say a word.

As he wrapped up the tour, guiding them toward the

hallway, he glanced back over his shoulder. Renata was still at the counter, talking to another guest, but her knowing gaze caught his for half a second. And just like that he knew the rest of the day would be just fine.

RENATA HAD NEVER felt more at home. She moved through the lodge like she'd been born to do this, welcoming guests, answering questions, anticipating what they needed before they even asked. Because this is what she did. Solved problems. Created warmth. Made people feel like they belonged. And today? Today, that skill felt like second nature.

She watched Gabe from across the dining hall, catching glimpses of him between conversations, guiding guests, answering questions, shaking off his nerves one interaction at a time. She was proud of him. Proud of how hard he had worked over the last week, making sure every last detail was perfect before the grand opening. She had seen his late nights, his early mornings, the weight he carried making sure this place wouldn't just open, but thrive.

Renata hadn't expected to feel this way. Not here, in Montana, not this settled, this sure. Because when she had first arrived, broken, uncertain, carrying wounds too deep to name, she never imagined this place could be her home. She had been running. From choices. From grief.

But Montana had given her space. Grace. A place to breathe when everything else had felt suffocating. And somehow, through long days, hard moments, unexpected joy, she had stopped running. She had built this, side by side with Gabe, step by step, until it was as much hers as it was his.

So when the food truck finally pulled in, late but not disastrous, Renata didn't hesitate. Because this was her home. And she knew exactly how to care for it. She strode out to meet them, directing the staff, ensuring the setup was smooth, moving across the property like she'd lived here for years.

And maybe, maybe in a way, she had. Not in time. But in belonging. Because this place was hers now. Not just Gabe's lodge, not just a job, not just a passing season. Hers. As the guests settled in, the dining hall came alive, and everything felt exactly right.

By the time the last echoes of the day's chaos faded, Renata sank into the plush lobby couch, Gabe beside her, both of them drawn toward the flickering glow of the fireplace. Heat from the flames seeped into her tired limbs, the soft crackle filling the dimly lit space, wrapping them in quiet. She sighed, nestling closer against Gabe's side, her head resting lightly on his shoulder. He was solid, carrying the faint scent of leather, soap, and the crisp pine-kissed air just beyond the lodge doors. She felt like she could sit here forever.

"I can't believe we survived today," Gabe murmured, his voice low, worn from hours of conversation, but lined with something close to amusement.

Renata let out a soft laugh. "Barely."

He huffed, rubbing a hand over his face. "I still think Miss Blair Everly was sent by God himself to keep me humble."

She grinned. "Oh, you handled her just fine."

He shook his head, stretching his legs out. "Yeah, but when her friend started—"

Renata nudged him lightly. "You handled her too."

His fingers brushed absently over hers where their hands rested between them. Then he whispered, "I'm glad I went to Vargas Guest Ranch back in the spring."

Renata turned slightly, lifting her head. Gabe kept his gaze on the fire, his jaw tight, like he was still reckoning with that truth himself.

"I remember walking into your office that day..." He huffed a quiet laugh. "You were eight months pregnant."

She smirked. "Shocking, I know."

His lips quirked slightly, but his expression held something deeper. "But I walked out that day different," he admitted. "I didn't realize it then, but—" He exhaled slowly. "God was setting up something I couldn't even see yet."

A warmth settled deep in her chest, something unspoken passing between them. She tucked herself closer, her fingers brushing gently over his forearm.

"You saved me, Gabe."

His breath hitched just slightly, his gaze flicking to her. She swallowed, staring into the fire. "I don't know what I would have done if you hadn't whisked me off to Montana."

His jaw tightened again, his grip firming slightly around her fingers. But he didn't speak, just listened. Renata exhaled softly. "I needed time to heal. And you gave me that."

Gabe studied her for a long moment, his thumb grazing over the back of her hand. Then, his voice low, warm, full of quiet reverence, he said, "You didn't just heal."

She turned toward him, pulse kicking slightly at the way he watched her now. "You became a Montana cowgirl."

She blinked. He grinned, shaking his head slightly. "Look at you," he mused, gesturing lazily toward her boots, her worn jeans, her snap-front shirt. The ease with which she moved through the ranch, belonged to it.

"When I met you, you were all polished Arizona resort manager," he continued. "Now you know how to saddle your own horse, run a ranch, and bake cookies under pressure. If that's not a Montana cowgirl, I don't know what is."

Renata laughed softly, warmth spreading through her chest at the way he said it, like it wasn't just a compliment. Like it meant something more. "You know, I could saddle a horse in Arizona, too."

He leaned in and nuzzled his nose against her neck, making it hard to think straight. "And I have been baking cookies since I was five."

His lips pressed against her neck. Her breath hitched as

tingles rolled through her limbs. Then his lips met hers, gentle, slow, soaked in exhaustion but rich in quiet gratitude. An exhale, a promise, a prayer without words.

She sighed against him, the warmth of his lips steadying her, grounding her in this moment, in this life she had chosen. Then a voice broke into their bubble.

"Oh, wow, sorry. I didn't mean to interrupt!"

Renata jerked back, her eyes flying open just as Blair Everly's friend stood two feet away, phone poised in her hands. Blushing furiously, Renata buried her face in Gabe's shoulder.

The woman grinned, clearly unbothered by catching them in a private moment. "You two make a lovely couple," she said, motioning to her phone. "Mind if I take a picture?"

Renata blinked, caught completely off guard as Gabe handed over his phone. "As long as you take one for us to keep."

The woman smiled and snapped a picture using Gabe's phone before handing it back. Then she held up her own. "How long have you been married?"

Renata sucked in a sharp breath, sputtering, scrambling for words, but Gabe didn't hesitate. "We're not."

Her pulse kicked hard. And then just one word, simple, confident, sent her dreams spinning. "Yet."

She turned toward him, breath caught in her ribs. He shifted slightly, his gaze steady and warm, carrying unspoken promise. "I hope to remedy that soon."

Everything settled then. This wasn't just another moment. It was every choice that had led her here, every fear faced, every uncertainty overcome, every quiet prayer she hadn't realized she was making.

She had thought Montana was temporary. But looking at Gabe now, at the certainty in his voice, at how his presence had steadied her, she knew it never had been.

God had always been leading to this. To Gabe. To her future. She hadn't come to Montana for love. But love had found her, anyway.

Epilogue

THE HIGHWAY STRETCHED long before them, winding south through Montana's sprawling beauty, fall's golden aspens glowing against the backdrop of endless blue sky. Renata shifted in her seat, gazing out at the passing landscape, the rhythm of Gabe's truck a steady hum beneath them.

"It feels surreal," she murmured, breaking the comfortable silence.

Gabe glanced at her, one hand resting on the steering wheel, the other draped loosely over the console between them. "What does?"

She exhaled, adjusting her seatbelt. "Leaving Montana. The lodge's first season is done. When we get back, we'll be prepping for winter."

He nodded, thoughtful. "We pulled it off, though. More than pulled it off."

She glanced at him, brow furrowing slightly. There was something in his voice, not just satisfaction, but relief. A deep, weight-off-his-shoulders kind of relief. Her pulse hitched, realization sparking. "Wait, you mean financially?"

Gabe's lips tugged into a slow, knowing smirk. "Exceeded projections. More than enough to get through winter. More than enough to keep the ranch running."

Something warm and unexpected bloomed in her chest. They had done it. Not just scraped by, not just barely held on. They had saved the Broken Spur. She turned back to the window, breathing in that truth, letting it settle deep in her ribs. They saved Gabe's ranch. Their ranch. Dare she hope?

The thought lingered, soft, thrilling, terrifying. She settled into the companionship of silence, the miles slipping by, and somewhere between the curves of the road, the nostalgia crept in. Arizona. Her old life. Her family. She felt a shift in her chest, something tightening, something pressing at the edges of her ribs.

Gabe noticed immediately. He flicked her a glance, one brow raised. "You're quiet."

She swallowed, fingers tracing idle patterns along the seam of her jeans. "Just thinking about my family."

He smirked slightly. "About Cliff?"

She huffed a laugh, shaking her head. "You really do know me, don't you?"

Gabe reached across the console, his fingers brushing hers just slightly. "Yeah. And I know this trip isn't just about packing up your apartment."

Her throat tightened. No. It wasn't. Because Cliff would be there. Laughing, thriving. A five-month-old reminder of everything she had lost and everything she had gained. And as they finally turned onto the familiar gravel road leading into Vargas Guest Ranch & Resort, she realized she was ready. For closure. For joy. For everything waiting on the other side of this weekend.

The late-afternoon Arizona sun cast long, golden shadows, stretching across the dry earth, painting Dalton Peak in deep amber hues. It stood tall, proud, a constant sentinel over the ranch her family had called home for more than seventy-five years. Four generations. And now, she was the first in her generation to leave. One of only two, ever.

The weight of that truth settled unexpectedly in her chest, pressing just slightly, like the heat radiating off the pavement. Yet, no doubts, no regrets. God had called her to Montana.

Gabe eased the truck to a stop near her apartment, cutting the engine. Renata sat there for a moment, staring at the front door, a door she hadn't walked through since she left for Montana months ago. Home. At least, it had been.

She inhaled deeply, catching the faint scent of mesquite and desert brush, then exhaled slowly before turning to Gabe. "I need a minute."

He nodded, his steady gaze holding hers. No questions, no pressure, just quiet understanding. As she stepped inside, memories rushed in, not painful, just present. The books stacked on the shelves, the framed photo of her parents, the scent of warm cotton, and the lumpy couch that had seen both joy and heartbreak.

She could almost hear Solana's laughter, the sharp hum of their whispered conversations, and the quiet sobs they had shared when life felt too heavy. And yet packing felt simple. Easy. Not painful. Because Montana was waiting. And Gabe was waiting.

By the time Sunday morning arrived, Renata felt ready. She stepped into the church, Gabe beside her. The faint scent of fresh coffee from the lobby hung in the air and the hum of quiet conversation. Familiar. Comforting. The rows of padded chairs filled the sanctuary, arranged for flexibility, a sign of their growing congregation and the evolving space that welcomed them.

She barely had time to breathe before her parents and sister appeared. Her mother's eyes lit up instantly, her father's quiet grin pressed deep into the lines of his weathered face.

"Mija!"

Her father pulled her into an extra-long embrace, his hand resting lightly on the back of her head, steady, comforting, just as he had done since she was a child. Her eyes burned at the tenderness, her chest tightening slightly. She had chosen a man of character. Just like her father.

Her sister, Solana, rushed forward, wrapping Renata in a tight, familiar squeeze. "You're finally home," Solana murmured, pressing her chin on Renata's shoulder for just a second longer than expected.

Renata hugged her back. Not just home. Home in a new way. She pulled back, eyes brightening instantly at the sight of Solana's round belly.

"Look at you!" Renata exclaimed, reaching instinctively for Solana's hands. "The glow. The baby bump. My little sister is going to be a mother!"

"Again," Solana laughed softly.

The word settled between them, a quiet reminder. Solana had become a stepmom the day she married Adan. Renata swallowed, warmth pressing deep in her ribs.

"Do you want all the maternity stuff from..."

Solana's features softened instantly. "No. But if it's boxed up, I'll have Adan donate it."

Renata nodded, grateful for the quiet understanding that had always existed between them. As they settled in for the service, Gabe was right beside her, absorbing everything. The hushed murmurs of prayer, the quiet reverence woven into every corner of the sanctuary, the subtle but unshakable foundation of faith that had shaped her family for generations.

And then, without a word, Gabe reached for her hand. Not dramatic. Not intentional for anyone but her. Just a quiet, grounding touch. Renata let out a slow breath, fingers tightening around his. Because he belonged here too. She could feel it.

The final song lingered in the air, voices rising in reverent harmony before settling into quiet murmurs as the congregation moved toward the doors. Renata stepped outside, the late-morning sun warm against her skin, casting sharp shadows across the courtyard.

Her father squeezed her shoulder lightly, his grip steady, familiar, grounding. "You coming straight to Catalina's?"

Renata nodded, adjusting her purse, casting a quick

glance toward Gabe, who had remained close throughout the service, silent but observant, absorbing everything. "I think I need food more than I need air right now," she teased.

Her mother chuckled. "Good thing Catalina made enough to feed an army."

She laughed, slipping her arm around Solana's as they walked toward their cars. Gabe fell into stride beside her, easy, unshaken by the whirlwind of family conversation already sparking around him. And as they pulled into Aunt Catalina's driveway, voices spilled from the open door, laughter threading through the space, and as Renata stepped inside, something deep within her settled completely.

She was home. Not the place. Not Arizona. This. This moment. These people.

The scent of smoked carne asada, fresh tortillas, and slow-simmered beans filled Aunt Catalina's house, wrapping around Renata like a familiar embrace. Voices rippled through the rooms, overlapping, teasing, catching up. Home. But something shifted as Devon and Raina approached. Cliff nestled against his mother's chest, his little fingers gripping the fabric of her blouse without a care in the world.

Renata felt it, the tightening in her chest, the awareness that this was the moment. Raina smiled widely, adjusting Cliff in her arms. "You wanna hold him?"

Renata hesitated. She hadn't held him, not even on that day. The day she brought him into the world. But now, standing here in the warmth of family, in the glow of laughter, something in her heart steadied.

Slowly, she lifted her arms. Raina placed Cliff gently in her grasp, his soft weight settling against her, the scent of baby lotion and warm skin filling the space between them.

Renata exhaled. No grief. No hesitation. Just joy. Pure, unshakable joy.

Cliff let out a giddy, easy laugh, kicking his tiny feet, his bright green eyes locking onto her as if he recognized something familiar, something safe. Renata smiled down at him, pressing a light kiss to his forehead, warmth and love blooming in her chest, deep, unwavering, completely sure.

"You were there the day he was born," Raina said warmly. "So it only seems right to introduce you properly." She adjusted Cliff's blanket, her voice filled with something more than gratitude, something honoring, something binding. "Meet your honorary aunt."

Renata swallowed. Her throat tightened, but not in grief. Not in loss. In acceptance. In peace. She laughed softly, nodding, feeling every remaining wound quietly, finally fade away.

From the corner of her vision, Gabe watched the exchange, his gaze steady, his expression unreadable but unmistakably present. And in that moment, this was it. The last piece. The final letting go of her past before her future unfolded completely.

THE SMOKY AND spicy aromas of carne asada, warm tortillas, and slow-simmered beans wafted through the house, filling every inch with the scent of home, of family, of something lived-in and whole. But Gabe barely registered it. Not when Renata held Cliff in her arms.

She had hesitated, just for a breath, just for a second, but the moment she adjusted him against her chest, something changed. The tension melted away, leaving only unfiltered joy. Her face lit, wholly unguarded, her smile soft, pure, unwavering, her eyes bright, fully present. No sorrow. No ache beneath the surface. Just Renata, fully here, fully happy.

She pressed a gentle kiss to Cliff's forehead, whispering something meant only for him, her voice barely audible over the hum of conversation, but Gabe felt it anyway, in the way

she held him, in the way her expression softened into something achingly certain.

This was closure. Not just for her. For them. Cliff giggled, kicking his tiny feet, and when Renata finally handed
him back to Raina, Gabe closed the space between them,
slipping in just enough so only she could hear him.

His voice came low, meant only for her, as his fingers
found hers between them, grounding, steadying, something
that felt like a promise before the promise. "You okay?"

Renata turned toward him, chest rising in a slow, steady
breath, as if she were releasing the last fragile strand of hesitation she hadn't realized she was still holding. She swallowed once, then smiled, soft, deep, unshakably sure. "Yes."

She curled her fingers around his instinctively, her touch
so natural, so effortless. It sent warmth settling deep into his
soul. She was really okay. And when her fingers tightened
just slightly, Gabe turned his palm upward, threading his
fingers through hers, anchoring them both to a love meant to
last.

She glanced up at him, a quiet flicker of a question in her
expression. He couldn't tell her yet. Not here. Not in a room
filled with conversation, filled with people, filled with everything but the quiet certainty of what he was about to ask her.
But soon. Very soon. Because the ring was in his pocket,
heavy with waiting, aching for her hand.

Renata pulled Gabe toward her brother-in-law, Adan,
and his teenage son, Jet. Adan waggled his eyebrows, stealing a glance at Gabe's pocket before leaning in just as Renata
moved on. "Everything's set."

Gabe nodded once, pulse kicking up slightly, before Renata called to him again, pulling him into another introduc-
tion. Her five cousins. Their wives. An entire army of babies
and kids running between chairs and slipping under tables.

Names blurred together, and Gabe barely had time to
keep track before dinner settled into deep conversation, stories spinning between bites of carne asada, warm rice, and

laughter. Renata, woven into all of it, glowing in the center of family, laughed easily, her joy unmistakable, effortless, fully present. And all Gabe could think about was the ring in his pocket, the weight of it pressing against his palm, the certainty of what came next. He couldn't even taste the food.

Renata nudged him gently, brow furrowing. "You've barely touched your food. Don't tell me Paco's bean burrito yesterday did you in."

A wan smile slipped onto his lips, his fingers pressing against the velvet box in his pocket. "Nothing like that." Not even close.

He waited. The conversation slowed, laughter softened, the din of voices settling just enough. Renata was glowing. And Gabe just sat in it for a beat, breathing her in, letting the assurance press deeper into his heart.

This wasn't just a moment. It was every moment before it, every hesitation, every step toward something unshakable, every time he had watched her walk toward joy instead of away from it. The ring was in his pocket. And she was ready.

And then, without hesitation, he pulled it out. The hum of voices stilled instantly. He dropped to one knee, hands shaking as he put his entire soul on display. For her.

"Marry me, Rennie."

Renata froze, her breath catching, eyes locking onto his, wide, unguarded, unfiltered. For half a second, he thought she might cry. Not out of shock. Not out of fear. But because this moment had waited for them, for both of them, for so long.

Her fingers twitched, hovering near her lips, as if she needed to steady herself, to hold back something overwhelming, something too big for words. Then, just barely, just softly, she exhaled. Not a sharp breath. Not a gasp. Something deeper. Something unraveling. Something anchoring.

Gabe swallowed hard. And then laughter slipped free,

shaking in her chest. Radiant, full, breathtaking in the best possible way. She reached for him before she even spoke, fingers curling instinctively around his wrist, like she had to feel him, had to ground herself in the truth of this moment before she could answer it.

Her chest rose, fell, her voice coming low, unsteady but unshakably sure. "Yes."

Not rushed. Not forced. Just a truth settling between their hearts. The room erupted, voices crashing into cheers, into celebration, into the full, uncontainable embrace of family and joy and faith.

Someone nudged one of her cousins, muttering, "That's how you do it."

Gabe didn't care. Because in that moment, it was her. It was them. It was everything. Renata was still watching him, something wet in her eyes, something achingly raw, something so deeply right, and he wanted to kiss her, so he did. Not rushed. Not hurried. Just a quiet press of certainty, of love, of everything they had ever been and everything they would be from this day forward.

THE HUM OF the truck rolled steadily beneath them, tires eating up the highway, the desert fading behind. Slowly, over their two-day journey, the scene gave way to Montana's golden fall fields. Renata sat beside Gabe, quiet. Not tense, not hesitant. Just soaking in the weight of everything that had happened. She was his now. Completely, fully, without hesitation.

Gabe adjusted his grip on the wheel, letting his gaze flick briefly toward her, catching the soft contentment in her expression, the lingering glow of laughter that had carried them through Sunday supper. Then, without thinking, without forcing it, he muttered, "We do not deviate from the

Lord's plan."

Renata's gaze slipped toward him, brow rising slightly, a knowing smile tugging at the corner of her lips. "The Vargas family motto," she murmured.

Gabe nodded. "It was written across the dining hall, right above the entry," he recalled. "I saw it every day when I was staying at the ranch."

Renata hummed softly. "Did you ever think about what it meant?"

Gabe huffed out a quiet chuckle, shaking his head slightly. "To be honest, I used to wonder if people read that phrase and heard something different from God."

She tilted her head, watching him. "Like what?"

He shrugged, fingers drumming lightly against the steering wheel. "Some might hear 'stay the course.' Others might hear 'go a new way.' Some might take it as a warning. Others as a reassurance."

Renata's lips pressed together in thought, nodding slightly. "I can see that."

He glanced toward her again, exhaling. "I think I expected God's plan to show up in an express mailer or a burning bush back when I first got to Arizona."

Renata laughed, warm, knowing, completely amused. "And instead," she teased, "it showed up in an eight-month pregnant resort manager."

Gabe smirked, reaching for her hand, threading his fingers through hers, anchoring them both in something solid. "Apparently," he admitted. "And I can't say it was a bad way for God to get my attention."

She squeezed his fingers, her gaze soft, certain. Gabe let himself sit in the quiet for a beat, the weight of it all settling into his chest, Montana's mountains rising ahead like a promise of something meant to be.

Then, softly, almost absently, he asked, "Think we need one of our own?"

Renata blinked, brow furrowing slightly. "A motto?"

Gabe nodded once, gaze still on the road. "You, me, our future. Seems like we should have one."

She was quiet for half a second. Then a soft, teasing laugh. "Starting our own traditions already?"

Gabe grinned. "Might as well."

She exhaled slowly, thoughtfully, before finally turning to him, her voice steady, sure. "We don't have to figure it out right now."

Gabe squeezed her hand again, nodding. Because they didn't. They had time. And more importantly, they had the certainty that God had already been guiding them forward. And that? That was more than enough.

Buried secrets. Lost stories.
A legacy waiting to be uncovered.

As Vargas Ranch prepares to celebrate eighty years, Devon Vargas embarks on a search for his family's true beginnings. But what starts as a simple dive into history soon unearths long-buried truths—pieces of a past tied to the founding couple, Dalton Sr. and Maria Vargas.

For Tres Vargas, these revelations collide with his own struggles, forcing him to reckon with the weight of faith, redemption, and the ties that bind generations together. As father and son piece together the letters, records, and hidden stories of their ancestors, they discover that legacy isn't just about where you come from—it's about the choices that shape the future.

When the truth is finally laid bare, will it strengthen their family bonds—or unravel everything they thought they knew?

A deeply moving family saga rooted in faith, honor, and the resilience of love, Falling for a Cowboy's Legacy weaves past and present into an unforgettable story of redemption and trust.

Get *Falling for a Cowboy's Legacy* as a gift when you sign up for my newsletter:

```
https://books.karenbaney.com/falling-
          for-a-cowboys-legacy
```

Find out:

- What's the secret behind the name Dalton Peak?
- How did the Vargas family motto come to define generations?

This novella uncovers the hidden history that shaped the Vargas family—don't miss this final chapter in the family saga!

From the Author

Surrogacy has long been part of conversations about family-building, yet it seems to slip in and out of public awareness. I remember when it was in the headlines decades ago, a topic of discussion, curiosity, even controversy. Then—just as quickly—it felt like something no one talked about anymore.

And yet, today, for couples navigating fertility challenges, surrogacy remains a profound and life-changing option. While estimates vary, it's believed that around 10,000 surrogate births occur in the U.S. each year—quiet reminders that this path to parenthood is still very much alive.

Like Renata, I sometimes find myself questioning whether I've heard God's gentle whispers right. And if I did—why am I in a season of grief or darkness? Why does the journey feel so hard? Renata's story reminded me of something I've needed to hold onto myself—God never promised easy or fair. But He did promise to be with us, in every moment, in every hardship, in every season of waiting.

In writing Renata's journey, I knew her story would carry emotional weight, especially for those who have experienced loss. Grief changes us. It reshapes our dreams, our expectations, even our faith. But hope? Hope remains. My deepest wish is that Renata's journey offers that—a reminder that healing takes time, but new chapters do come.

Speaking of new chapters—don't miss Falling for a

Cowboy's Legacy! Be sure to sign up for my newsletter to get updates, sneak peeks, and exclusive content. I'd love to stay connected with you as these characters continue to unfold.

Thank you for taking this journey with me to Vargas Guest Ranch & Resort. And keep an eye out for new series Love at Vargas Ranch!

Blessings,

Karen Baney

About the Author

Karen Baney is passionate about writing stories full of flawed characters. She enjoys weaving together stories of second chances, redemption, and overcoming personal trials. As a transplant to Arizona, she loves researching the state's history and finding ways to seamlessly incorporate real history and real settings into her novels. In addition to writing and speaking, Karen works as a Software Development Manager for a Christian ministry.

Her faith plays an important role both in her life and in her writing. Karen and her husband, Jim, make their home in Gilbert, Arizona, with their two dogs, Bella and Daisy. Both Jim and Karen are active at Rock Point Church in Queen Creek, Arizona.

Discover faith-laced stories with characters who feel like lifelong friends.

Visit www.karenbaney.com to discover more historical romance series set in the American West. Follow Karen's writing journey and get behind-the-scenes glimpses of her research adventures on social media.

Facebook: @AuthorKarenBaney
X: @karen_baney
Instagram: @AuthorKarenBaney
BookBub: Follow Karen Baney for new release alerts

Books By Karen Baney

<u>Contemporary Romance</u>

Vargas Ranch Series:
Love is in the air at the Vargas Guest Ranch & Resort near Wickenburg, Arizona. Meet the Vargas family—five swoon-worthy brothers and their cousins who live by their family motto: "We do not deviate from the Lord's plan." These rugged cowboys run a successful working ranch and luxury resort while navigating the rollercoaster of finding true love.

Falling for a Fake Cowboy
Falling for a Real Cowboy
Honeymoon with a Real Cowboy
Falling for a Shy Cowboy
Falling for a Bossy Cowboy
Falling for a Smart Cowboy
Falling for a Humbug Cowboy
Falling for a Devoted Cowgirl
Falling for a Pregnant Cowgirl
Falling for a Cowboy's Legacy

Steadfast Love Series:
The *Steadfast Love* series follows a close-knit group of friends as they navigate the beautiful mess of modern life in the Phoenix area—workplace drama, complicated families, and love that shows up when they least expect it. These contemporary romances blend emotional depth with authentic faith, reminding us that even when life unravels, God's love never does.

The Heart I Rescue (prequel)
The Air I Breathe

Historical Western Romance

Prescott Pioneers Series:

Step back in time to the wild, untamed Arizona Territory where survival depends on grit, faith, and the courage to start over. Follow three pioneer families—the Andersons, Colters, and Larsons—as they risk everything for the promise of a new life in a land that demands both strength and hope.

A Dream Unfolding
A Heart Renewed
A Life Restored
A Hope Revealed
Hidden Prospects

Desert Manna Series:

Sometimes the most beautiful love stories bloom in the desert. Set in the growing frontier town of Prescott during the early 1870s, these tender romances follow women rebuilding their lives after heartbreak and the unexpected men who help them discover that second chances at love are worth the risk. Set in Prescott, Arizona between 1871 - 1873.

Beauty for Ashes
Joy for Mourning
Oaks of Justice

Colter Sons Series:

Power, legacy, and forbidden love collide in this sweeping family saga set in the Arizona Territory. The Colter ranch empire has weathered decades of frontier life, but now family secrets and buried betrayals threaten to destroy everything. As five brothers—and one resilient sister—navigate the treacherous waters of love, loss, and redemption, they must decide what's worth fighting for. Set in Prescott and other locations within the Arizona Territory in 1887 - 1906.

The Reluctant Cattleman
The Roaming Adventurer
The Railroad Magnate
The Resourceful Stockman
The Restless Wrangler
The Resilient Bride

<u>Larson Sisters Series</u>
Meet the next generation! These delightful novellas follow the three daughters of Adam and Julia Larson from the *Prescott Pioneers Series* as they navigate love, courtship, and finding their own happily ever afters in territorial Arizona in 1886 – 1894.

In Love at Christmas
In Love with the Rancher
In Love with the Horse Trainer

Desert Life Media

Desert Life Media: *There Is Life in The Desert*

Entertainment-first Christian fiction set in the Southwest, featuring redemption, family, and faith

Publishing clean, wholesome, and uplifting fiction since 2010

---

desertlifemedia.com

www.ingramcontent.com/pod-product-compliance
Lightning Source LLC
Chambersburg PA
CBHW071902220626
47052CB00002B/176